A HARD FALL

G. L. KAUFMANN

A HARD FALL

MULBERRY PUBLISHING

MULBERRY PUBLISHING

Published by Mulberry Publishing 2018
Copyright © G.L. Kaufmann

First Published in Great Britain in 2018 by
Mulberry Publishing, London

www.mulberrypublishing.co.uk

British Library Cataloguing-in-Publication Data
A catalogue record for this book is available from the British Library

ISBN 978-1-9993041-0-2

Typeset in 9/12pt Dante by Fakenham Prepress Solutions
Printed and bound by Clays Ltd, Elcograf S.p.A.

Cover by Mecob Design Ltd

For my father who believed in England

Minus Seven: Monday

A massive, buttressed structure rose up on a podium, silhouetted against bright stadium lights. Steve recognised the outline from some deep hidden memory. He had only ever seen gallows in games, films and comic books. He flicked his mouse to increase the volume on the NBBC News.

'...rapidity with which the Act has come into force has been praised by the Prime Minister. He will be attending the first public execution next Monday. The name of the first convict to be executed has not been announced.'

He was going to have to watch that live. It wouldn't matter if it was during work hours, it would be patriotic to watch. It would be cool. It was quite technical; they had to get the fall right to break the neck otherwise people would kick around for an age. Quick deaths were what you wanted. A long agonising death might play on viewers' sympathies. You did not want the crowd getting maudlin.

He needed to pee. He got up. He rubbed his eyes, it was late. He took a step forward and felt something soft give underfoot. A pizza box. He had missed the crust. He kicked the box aside. There were definite advantages to living alone, no one telling you when to clear up was a good example. Mind you, even he could see that there were more cans of Pepsi, and greasy pizza and fish and chip boxes scattered around the room than was anyone's idea of good housekeeping. His mum would say it was squalid, so he made sure she never came to see him.

A two-room apartment might have been better, but a studio was all he could afford and even that had taken years to save up for. After Birmingham had become the capital of Britain, it was the one place to escape the crash in property prices that had affected the remainder of the country. The only person who had ever seen the squalor was Daenerys of the House Targaryen, the First of Her Name, The Unburnt, Queen of the Andals, the Rhoynar and the First Men, Queen of Meereen, Khaleesi of the Great Grass Sea, Protector of the Realm, Lady Regnant of the Seven Kingdoms, Breaker of Chains and Mother of Dragons to anyone else. She looked down over his bed, naked except for three newly hatched dragons. The edges of the poster were worn, the corners curled up and frayed; he had hung it in every room he had slept in since for ever. He worshipped her. Dany.

With the sound of the toilet still flushing he slumped down, rubbing his eyes. He glanced at the news, the gallows were gone. There was an analogue clock ticking away in the top right-hand corner of the monitor. It was seventeen minutes past three, well past bed-time. He liked that clock. It was the only old-fashioned thing that he had, but even that was digital. He had three monitors, but that was not enough. He had split the right screen in two, like the country. It was permanently tuned to the news. He had New BBC News on the left side and, under the clock, was the London News. That was strictly illegal. It was just as well that he knew what he was doing; he had had to ring fence himself, cover his tracks with proxy IP addresses, SSL encryption, routing through TOR, multiple identities and fake logins. He did not want to end up in a police cell, he knew too well what would happen if he was caught. Research was not a defence.

The LBC news was showing huge cargo boats being unloaded in London. The reporter was black. Typical. He sounded English enough, surprisingly.

'...*dockworkers worked hard to unload the first shipment of goods since the new treaty with the EU came into effect. The dependence on trade with New Britain and the punitive tariffs imposed by Birmingham will be mitigated as the lower trading tariffs in the new Treaty come into effect...*'

Typical! We got the blame for charging them too much. It was the usual propaganda. They would see who needed who. Londoners, what had they got to do with the country? They produced nothing. They were like leeches sucking the farmers and manufacturers dry.

The middle screen was the important one, that was his gaming monitor. He had built it himself to the highest specifications. It had fantastic resolution and colours. The one on the left was theoretically his work one. He logged into his BiG Home Security server account, just to keep tabs. He had a mike and webcam set up on it (theoretically so he could work from home). In practice, it was for pleasure; he was a member of quite a few chatrooms as well as a consumer of porn. He only switched the left-hand monitor to work when he wasn't using it for its primary purpose.

Right now, there was a frozen image of Candyxxx15, at least a screen shot of her finger on her nipple. It's not that he liked young girls – there was no way that Candy was the young side of 20 – but the personality that the so-called school girls projected was less threatening. Women, real women, were, well, real. The screen was like the one-way windows they used in the interrogation rooms at work. He reached his finger to the glass and stroked the smooth, surface over her nipple. His finger smeared a trail through the dust over the flat, lifeless screen.

Back to the game. He was running the police department in a lousy, crime-ridden American city. There were drug gangs, people traffickers and general villainy to deal with and a corrupt police force. The criminal mastermind was dangling a hostage, a small child, over the edge of the eighteenth floor of an office block building site. It was a long way down. Either he let the criminal go with the child, or he shot the criminal and the child would die. Not his favourite choice, but he favoured Spock's logic. If the thug got away he would probably kill the kid and carry on killing others; one death was worth many lives saved, however innocent and blue-eyed the child. He shot the criminal. Choices, choices maketh a man. He walked to the edge of the building and looked down. The criminal mastermind and child lay unmoving in a pool of blood. He clicked on Shut Down. Time for bed.

Maisie stood up. God! Her back hurt. This picking thing was mad. It was months now but still each day was exhausting. Fucking tomatoes. Fucking asparagus. And now Fucking strawberries. She used to get all her food from Iceland and she had never heard the word 'seasonality' before. Not then, not when the UK had still been the UK, before it had dis-united. In those days she had lived on benefits. She had voted Leave, like everyone she knew. 'Coming over and taking our jobs.' Yeah, that's what they had all mumbled. She had never thought it through, if They didn't do the work, who would? Anyone on fucking benefits, that's who. Muggins like her.

So here she was on her knees in a poly-tunnel in the Weald, wherever the hell that was, while her kids were at home with her mum over in Thanet. She'd had enough juice and credit on her phone to ring last night and her mum had said she would take them to Westgate Beach. God, she had loved that beach when she was a kid, the sea going out for ever, all them pools and tiny changing rivulets to play in, more mud than sand really but she hadn't cared. They had always hankered after having one of those beach huts, all nicely painted with old couples sitting out front on their la-de-da reclining beach chairs, Home Sweet Home mugs of tea steaming, plates of digestives. Now this; bent over all day snapping strawberries off the plants.

She had baulked when the coach had dropped them at the field at 5:15 that morning. No table tops. In all the other fields strawberries grew on table tops, but according to Darcy, her team leader, the farm had run out of money for modernisation after Brexit because labour costs had shot up. She wasn't exactly raking it in so that didn't figure. Darcy had muttered something about the picking rates going down and needing more people. That had to be crap; like she was meant to believe that the Poles or Bulgarians worked harder for less? Were they super-human or something? Whatever. This field had never got to be converted and it was doing her back in bending over all day.

The rota worked out so that they only came here once a week. Her back hurt from bending over the bushes on the ground, she was sweating in the super-heated poly-tunnel and she did not dare take her top off. She couldn't work out if it was because she was too ashamed of the roll of fat on her belly when she bent over. It was not like any of the guys looked at her, they were all too busy picking but being invisible was worse than being gawped at. She got back down and knelt by the next bush. El-bloody-santa. She knew all the varieties now. What you got to know when opportunity knocked. Last year, a strawberry was a strawberry. Now she didn't eat Elsanta, didn't rate Sweet Evie or a Sonata, was happy with Driscoll Jubilee or Amesti but give her a poly-tunnel of Malling Centenary, and she would pick them with a tender care that she reserved for her kids. When she had started she had eaten lots of fruit destined for the bin at the bottom of her table-top trolleys. Now she was more discerning; she ate only the Malling Centenary and Driscoll berries that were too ripe to pack. Although today it might make more sense to eat the Elsanta, rather than fill the effin sledge she had to shunt along.

She stripped the bush of all the red fruit, the good fruit went into the punnets. The big berries were going into the M&S punnets and the smaller ones into the Tesco ones; they were all fussy. One inch here, 1 $^3/_8$ there, and the big 1 $^5/_8$ ones over there. And that was another bloody thing, she had grown up with millimetres and centimetres and now they had bloody gone and returned to the Victorian age and inches and feet. It was daft. Twelve inches in a foot and three of them in a yard. And the inches were divided into eighths? That was one thing that it had been mental to throw out. She chucked the spoilt fruit into the bin under her sledge, left the hard, green ones alone and shuffled onto the next plant. It was back-breaking, literally; bring back the Poles, please. She looked up, Darcy was helping the new girl who had started yesterday. She was leaning over the bushes, no t-shirt, her breasts dangling in her stretchy comfort bra. She slowed, some people could pick fast and chat and watch, she couldn't. Darcy was always going on about the bleedin' picking rate, but it was slower here pushing the sledge stacked with the trays and punnets on the ground. In the table-top fields they had trolleys with enormous thick tyres, like mountain bikes, here it was archaic. Darcy stood up.

'Heh, Darcy.'

She was about twenty, pale, freckled and hard-working. There was something serious about her. More than Maisie had been at that age; she wouldn't have been a mum twice over at twenty if she had had her head screwed on like Darcy. That's why Darcy was the team leader and she was not.

'Yeah.'

'Don't you feel a bit exposed?'

'It's really hot.'

'What about Tom?'

'He's too obsessed with the picking rates to give me the once over.'

'He can't keep his eyes off you.'

'Really? What's he going to do; sack me for getting my tits out?'

'No, but he might try something.'

'So what? He's nothing I can't handle. He knows it's against farm regulations; you know, management can't mess with the teams.'

Maisie looked up at the white plastic ceiling. She knew the sky was blue, but inside here even the sun was just a white disc. She pulled her own t-shirt over her head.

'Don't laugh.'

'What are you worried about. No one cares. Look at the guys – they're all doing it.'

Two hours later they were back at the camp, sitting on a bench under a tree drinking the ice tea that Darcy had made the night before. She seemed to know stuff like that. Make a cup of tea, pick some herbs from the farm garden the other side of the hedge, add in some waste strawberries from the field and the next day, just when you needed it, the best drink in the world and for the price of one tea bag.

They had stopped at one. You can't pick strawberries when the sun's been shining on them; they're not as good and spoil. Jane and Amy, who shared the other bunk in their hut, had headed straight for the showers. Before the other teams got back. Maisie felt too tired to move and too dehydrated to even need to pee.

'I'm going to catch me some sun.'

'You're going to sunbathe?'

'Yeah, I like a tan.'

'But?'

Darcy shot her a filthy look that cut her off. She was right, when she was younger she would have been on Westgate Beach every weekend soaking up the sun, trying to get bronzed. Then all of a sudden white, lily white, was the new rage, everyone scuttling away from the sun. Sure, the huge posters after the crash out of the Brexit negotiations had only ever mentioned skin cancer, but the vibe caught on. White was good, it was a pass, through road blocks, stop and search and being hassled by the police for anything.

She picked up her phone and dialled. No answer. Her mum had probably left the phone at home. She was being paranoid; the kids would be fine, at least these two.

Jenny looked up from her screen; at least she gave the semblance of looking at the BVD/032a Form on display. Her eyes darted either side of the frame and over; no one was looking. At the top right-hand corner, she could see her webcam's image of herself in a superimposed mini-window. She looked back at herself – long soft brown hair, hazel eyes and, most importantly, pale skin. 'It's the first thing they see,' the trainer had told her when she had joined the Britishness Verification Department (*'BVD we aim to please!'* – how she loathed the greeting she had to answer the BiG phone or video calls with.) 'It means they know they are in safe hands, hands they can trust, when they see who you are.' When they see you're white is what the trainer had meant.

She double clicked on the tiny square, it instantly exploded to full screen. It was handy, she could check over her shoulder without turning: the coast was clear, no one was around. She double clicked again, her image shrank. Question 6 was spread in four columns across the page. One for each grandparent. She selected BRITISH for the first three. Then for the maternal grandmother she let the cursor hover over her choices. BRITISH, MIXED, FOREIGN. Blink. Blink. She selected MIXED. Another window dropped down, with two columns: a list of races down the left and in the right-hand column space for typing in the appropriate percentage: AFRICAN, ANGLO-SAXON, ASIAN – Other, AUSTRALASIAN – Aboriginal, CELTIC, COLONIAL – Other, COLONIAL – White, EUROPEAN, HONG KONG, HUGUENOT, INDIAN, JEWISH, LATIN AMERICAN, NORMAN, ROMA, ROMAN, VIKING. Thankfully the woman in question had not been gene tested, so Jenny did not have to fiddle about filling in the percentages. The one thing she had learned was that there was no such thing as pure British. Though if a Sicilian married a Dane, for example, they would, in fact, have a fairly typical British genetic mix.

She glanced down at the A4 sheet in front of her. The woman had brown eyes, brown hair. To be verified as British you had to either have a genetic profile demonstrating 75% Britishness (which is how people from South Africa and other colonies claimed citizenship) or all your foreign ancestors had to have come to Britain more than one hundred years ago – the Hundred Year Rule. She clicked on the box next to EUROPEAN and typed in '50' and the same next to INDIAN. She grandmother could be Anglo-Indian; the woman would be an octaroon. She was verifiable. ENTER. It was ironic the way they had returned to colonial categories; Pakistan, Bangladesh and India all re-united on the form as Britain itself fell apart.

She picked up her pen, wrote the same on the paper form and slipped it into a dog-eared manila folder. Then she slid the file under a pile of other tattered manila folders on the desk. She hit some keys, the screen changed into code. For a few seconds she tapped, removing all trace of her alterations from the system. Cover your tracks; that had been the mantra at the software training she had had with the Resistance when she had first signed up.

She returned to the BVD/032a form screen. NEXT.

The next form appeared. The face was brown, dark brown. There was nothing she could do about this one. She drew out the folder. Three children. Third generation in England. There was nothing to be done. The rule was if you were over eighteen and economically independent and third generation born here you could apply for citizenship. For automatic citizenship six out of eight great-grandparents had to come from British Ethnic stock or have been resident a 100 years ago. This family had no hope. They had only been here 70-odd years.

As for what Britishness was, that was a bureaucratic nightmare. There was some irony in this situation; people had blathered on about casting off that Brussels red-tape. But then no one had seen the British Nationality Act 2022 coming. Everyone had to be Verified British or Verified Not British. VB or VNB, that 'N' changed your life. Gene testing was mandatory but, while it was being rolled out, there was an opportunity for a few people like her to sabotage the process. She could class people as British when they were not and she could warn them when they were targeted by Re-Migration Services. Until everyone's genetic profile was on the national data base there was scope for action.

Luckily the process was slow. Like in many industries, the flight of foreign born technicians combined with the incompetent management of the local talent meant that the Britishness Verification Department was like a tanker drifting without an engine under its own momentum; a behemoth of inefficiency. Whatever they had chucked out, the New British Government, or BiG (His Majesty's Government had favoured NBG as an acronym but the political slogan *Britain is Great* reduced to BiG had caught on), seemed rife with its own new red tape. Jenny wondered whether Londoners or the Scots were as dogged by bureaucracy.

At one on the dot Jenny logged off for her lunch break. She did not bother saving her work, that was automatic, everything she did was logged, recorded and monitored. All BiG employees had biometric microchip implants. She swiped her wrist over the microchip reader as she left to sit in the park and have a sandwich. This action would put her PC into sleep mode.

Later she swiped her wrist to get back into the office; as the door opened, a message was sent to her PC. The screen would be ready when she sat back down. Big Brother had nothing on BiG.

As she returned to her desk, Meg at the next work station stood up.

'How's it going?' Jenny said, to be polite.

'Fine, just the usual. What's the weather like?'

'Lovely.'

Meg moved away.

Jenny swept three files into her briefcase for later. She could not put the original files into the trash, it was checked. She had to take the them home for shredding. Norman had the best shredder on the market. He was always laughing about the paper trails people left.

BiG Home Security Agent, Norman Marshall, came off at the roundabout and followed the slip road up to the gates. It was impossible to see into the Ashford Re-Migration Transit camp, the road was lined with hoardings depicting cricket games, country villages and white smiling faces. A man on a ladder was painting an image of Queen Victoria. The rest of the panels had not been painted yet, the bare aluminium sheets glistened in the sun.

Soldiers were standing sentry on either side of a barrier. There were another two in a booth. A tangle of barbed wire, rolls of thorns and spikes, like the rose bushes surrounding Sleeping Beauty, ran along the inside of the perimeter road. Each time he saw the mass of tents filling what had been the car park it reminded him of the time he had done security at Glastonbury. The festival tents had been erected haphazardly but these were in a martial array; neat rows of canvas running up and down. It was only six o'clock, the sun was still high, but there was no sign of life. This was no festival.

'Evening, sir?'

'Norman Marshall, to see the camp director.'

The sentry looked down at his clipboard.

'Yes, sir, you're on the list.'

He turned and shouted something to the man in the booth. The barrier lifted Norman drove round the inner-ring road, pulling up at the far end.

The Ashford Transit camp was the least worst one in the country. When BiG's work had gotten up steam it became clear that transit camps were needed everywhere, immediately. Ashford's Designer Outlet was perfect, an almost entirely enclosed ring of buildings with a large open space (the former car park) in the middle and only two entrances and exits to man at either end once all the external doors had been sealed – a modern-day fortress.

Gap, Le Creuset, Nike, Levis, all closed-up shop. After London declared UDI, there was no one coming down by train anymore to shop and most of the sales assistants were either hunkered down in London or on their way back home across the Channel. The army moved in, erected the tents and then the re-migrants were brought in. Ashford was efficient. They arrived, they were processed and with luck they would be put on trains within a week. At first the border control in Paris and Brussels tried to keep them on the trains, then the platforms, but eventually they had to let the human tide out as Britain spat out its unwanted aliens onto their streets.

He took out his mobile, placed a call and waited.

'I'm here.'

A few moments later a light came on behind the glass front. Despite being backlit he could make out the letters 'Superdry'. Ironic he thought, a slight figure came to the door and unlocked it.

'Norman, thank God,' Tess said. She was wearing a sharp suit, her hair pulled back tight in a bun. She looked too good to be the camp director.

'Who is it this time?'

'Lord David Samson.'

'Not another peer.'

'I know.'

'What's the issue?'

'We've given him the Declaration and shown him the British Verification form but he will have none of it.'

'Meaning?'

'He says, that despite being British through and through – Radio 4 vibrates through his body – that he is also fifty percent Hungarian Jew. His father came in 1936, served in the Pioneer corps, got a commendation, but he does not make the Hundred Year Rule. Samson got the peerage as a reward for campaigning to leave. He's the Earl of Beaconsfield.'

'And his mother?'

'Her maiden name is St John Danvers. Pure bred English rose.'

'Fuck.'

When he was done, he sat in the empty shop front and waited for Tess. It had taken him a while to work out why she was so well turned-out compared to all the other camp directors; most of the stores had been evicted overnight and their stock left behind. Tess had declared that the goods would be used for bettering the lives of those in transition and, of course, herself and her staff.

Tess appeared with a mug of steaming tea.

'So, did he agree? Did he sign?' She asked as she handed him the mug.

'Yes, he agreed. His signature is a bit smudged. He got a bit wet.'

Waterboarding was very effective. Everyone broke. No exception. Another national treasure saved. Propaganda was important, it was the way they fought London now.

He did not particularly like his job but it had to be done. He had learned, in Iraq and then again in Afghanistan, what it meant for a country to fall apart at the seams. He had no taste for violence; he just did not care. Seeing the carnage inflicted by suicide bombers in city centres had inured him to human screams and wails. The mewling of the cat he had bought Jenny was more affecting.

'Are you going back to Birmingham?'

He thought about it. He was not desperate to get home. Jenny was still angry most of the time. He'd given her the kitten in the hope that would make things better. Debs, her sister, slit her wrists in the bath after her husband and children had died. The Government had commandeered a fleet of cruise liners, stuffed them with VNBs from Asia and Africa and sent them out to sea with their Filipino crews. A few had made it to the sub-continent, some of the African ones had been commandeered by pirates, but Debs's family's boat had been torpedoed by the Pakistani navy. The judicial enquiry resolved that there had been a misunderstanding or break down in communications. It was a fuck-up. And then to cap it all Jenny's mum needed constant care and now she couldn't share that with Debs.

Tess twiddled the wisp of hair by her ear lobe. He loved Jenny, no question, but that was different from wanting to go home to her now. Last week he had fucked Tess in her office, but it had not been comfortable.

'I'm not in a rush.'

'Is your place far?'

The phone was ringing as Jenny walked into the flat. Norman knew her habits well. She picked up the phone. The screen confirmed that it was him.

'Hello love, I've just got in.'

'I guessed you would be getting home now.'

'Will you be back for dinner?'

'No, something's come up. I've got more to do down here with the Camp Director.'

She put the phone down. How dumb did Norman think she was? There was no point taking her jacket off now, she had no time to lose. She booted up his PC. The cat rubbed himself against her legs. She reached down to stroke it, waiting for the computer to boot up. The thing about most people is that they were unthinking, if not stupid; she tapped in his password. Microsoft made it easy. His office was virtual now, everything was in his diary, his emails, all brought up to date from whatever appliance he was on over the cloud. She checked his diary. He had just entered in a new appointment with Camp Director Webb at six. He would be shagging that bitch for an hour and then have a bite to eat. That gave her three to four hours tops. The roads were much faster now that there were almost no European lorries (the official line was this was a result of the Buy British Campaign but where were the British lorries?) Petrol was expensive; most people only made essential journeys. Bloody hell! She used to pop out in the car and drive half a mile and back for a pint of milk. That was unthinkable now. People plotted their journeys with care, accumulating several tasks for one outing. She checked Norman's emails for incoming jobs. She had to be disciplined about that, no short cuts, however boring it was logging onto the online server, she must not read the messages in Outlook. He would notice. She printed out two sheets, two profiles. Two hours forty minutes.

Birmingham was easier to get around now. Her car sped through the streets. She did not check her mirror to see if she was being followed, she would have noticed the lights of any car in the dark. But there were no lights, no traffic. The Asians and Afro-Caribbeans had all been holed up in Wolverhampton; the city was empty. Even moving the government to Birmingham had not made much impact. Anyway, with her official car no one would stop her. Whichever civil servant had had the foresight to move ministerial cars over to electric fuel had been a genius, her electric car zipped along silently.

She parked the car outside Mark's house and waited. Come on, get going girl. She had two hours and five minutes. She opened the car door. The air was cool. She should have worn a cardigan. She rang the doorbell. Mark took his time but when he saw her on the doormat he stepped out and pulled her into an embrace. She hugged him back as she felt his tongue parting her lips and flicking round her mouth. Once inside they both wiped their mouths.

'Does it have to be quite so authentic?' Jenny said as she wiped her hand over her skirt.

'If I'm meant to be having an affair with a colleague, it's got to look passionate.'

'OK,' she stared at him, 'I've got two more. We've got a couple of days to warn them.'

Mark led the way into his kitchen. He opened a cupboard and took down a pack of Rice Krispies and a second of cornflakes. He brought the cornflakes to the kitchen table and opened it. He unfurled the rim of the plastic bag and tipped over the box. A sheaf of papers slid onto the table.

'These came yesterday. Drone delivery.'

Jenny picked them up and leafed through them. There were ten BVD/032a Forms. *Verified Not British* had been stamped in red across the white space at the top of each page. Four came from one family – a father and his three children; an old man; a middle-aged woman; two ancient crone-like sisters. The last were two kids, aged ten and twelve, they had an additional stamp of DO. *Dis-Owned* was an official status now. Sometimes there was only one surviving parent, the mother's date of death in this case had been fifteen months before, and the father must have been *Verified British* (VB). He had signed them over for deportation, the BVD/033d Form was stapled alongside a copy of the mother's death certificate.

They had to choose. They had twenty-four hours to act. Twenty-four hours to find one of these families, warn them and get somewhere for them to go. But it was getting harder and harder. The Irish route was blocked up and the Scots had closed the border. At first the Scots had taken in everyone claiming asylum, but they had been overwhelmed and when non-British ethnic refugees started dying in droves over winter the Scots had promptly closed the border to avoid a humanitarian crisis. Or so they said. The fence they had built was closely guarded and controlled by the Pict Border Police; the blue-kilted, blue-helmeted, blue-faced uniform inspired fear in most. The Scottish media had made a big fuss about returning to Gaelic roots; blue had always been the national colour and had kept the Romans out.

'We'll have to choose the kids. They're pretty, they'll pass for white, no one would know any better.'

'And the family. The kids look white.'

'Yeah, but the dad? Look at his eyes and hair, he would never pass.'

'Would he let them go?'

They called it the miniature railroad; like the kinder transport and the underground railroad that helped Jewish children and African Americans escape the Third Reich and slavery. All they knew was that if they got a child to the Deacon and her husband at St Christopher's, they would pass them along the railroad through Wales and on to Ireland or find someone to adopt them. It was not as hard as they thought it would be. Many families had been torn apart that there were almost queues of bereft parents looking to care for someone, in the vague hope that someone somewhere in Europe or Scotland or Ireland would do the same for their own child.

'Let's try him.'

Twenty-eight minutes later they pulled up outside a run-down block of flats. Nineteen sixties concrete, decades of stains and leaks streaking over the grey. The lift was not working but they were only going to the fifth floor. Could have been worse, ten floors worse.

'Why do they always piss in the stairwell?' Mark said.

Jenny was panting slightly as she pushed the door onto the fifth-floor landing. It moved slowly.

'Needs oil.' Mark was not good at silence.

The door to number 54 was that shade of blue that was only found on council house doors. A cold, solid unhappy blue that was never seen without chips and dents. The aluminium letterbox was broken. There was a brown envelope fixed on the inside; it shivered with each gust of wind.

'Hard times!'

Jenny knocked on the door. She did not even try the doorbell; it was held together by flaking Sellotape.

Thud! Thud! Thud!

Ro froze. Someone was knocking on the door. The only people who called unannounced were officials. Three knocks was about right. Friends and family seemed to knock once or twice.

The manila envelope, which he had taped to the letterbox to keep the draught out, moved.

'Hello?' a woman's voice came through the opening.

Thud! Thud! Thud!

'Dad?'

Kiran was standing in his doorway, clutching the doorframe. He looked terrified.

'Keep your brother and sister in the bedroom. And shut the door.'

Kiran disappeared, shoving the door with his shoulder to shut it properly. The flat was a dump. Everything was broken. The three kids had to share a single room. The other bedroom had a huge dark patch in one corner and smelled of mildew. He approached the door.

'Hello? Rohan Dhillon?'

'Who's there?'

'We've come to help you. You have twenty-four hours before Re-Migration comes.'

Re-Migration. Fuck. Ro knew they would come sooner or later. He could get the kids out the back window, there was a flat roof over the garage, they could knot the sheets together to get them down.

'Who did you say you were?'

'We didn't. We can't.' We. She was not alone.

'How do I know that you're not Re-Migration?'

'Re-Migration would have hammered this door down by now.'

The door was on the latch, but he still jammed his foot against it before opening it a crack. He was taking no chances. There were two of them: the woman and a man. He could not see any others, but they could be out of sight.

'Can you help?'

'Yes, but it's not safe,' the man said, 'not for us, out here.'

'People talk,' the woman said.

Ro closed the door and pressed his head against it. It was true, Re-Migration services did not need to lie their way into people's homes. He unfastened the chain and opened the door. They came in wordlessly. The man shut the door. He was tall, broad-shouldered, ruggedly handsome and shiny clean. His blue suit looked sharp. The woman was also in work clothes, a silky blouse, her trousers and jacket hung well over her lean frame, her blond hair was tied back in a bun, she could have been forty or fifty, it was hard to judge. Ro did not know what Re-Migration agents would look like but these two did not seem aggressive enough. They stood facing him, their backs to the door.

'Who are you?'

'We can't tell you that. That's not how this works,' the woman said. 'We're here to help you; it puts us in danger too. You can't know who we are.'

'Look.' The man pulled some papers from his inner jacket pocket. He unfolded them. 'You're Rohan Brendan Dylan formerly Dhillon, D-H-I-L-L-O-N?' The man spelled out his father's Sikh surname; fat lot of good changing his name by deed poll to the Celtic spelling had done him.

'Yes.'

'Do you know what this form is?' The man waved the piece of paper at him. His passport photo was on the top corner.

'No,' he said shaking his head.

'It's a BVD/032a Form; see that VNB stamped in red across the top?'

'Yes.'

'That's just been processed. As my friend said, you have twenty-four hours before that door is smashed open.'

'How do you know?'

'We can't tell you,' the woman said, 'we are here to warn you that you'll be picked up the day after tomorrow. Your flat will be watched from tomorrow night. If you want out, if you want help, we've got twenty-four hours to get you out and on the railroad.'

'Re-Migration doesn't ask nicely.'

Ro leaned back against the wall. He closed his eyes and took a deep breath.

'Trust us. It's your kids' only chance,' the woman said, 'I know.'

There was something in the way she said that, something in her eyes. If what they said was true where could they go?

Kirsty's mum would not take them in. His mum had gone back to Ireland just after it was reunified.

'You had better come in.'

He led them into the kitchen. The man laid out the four forms, like a deck of cards, on the table.

'This is your family?'

'Yes. Well, me and the kids.'

'Do you mind if I sit?' the man said.

'Go ahead.'

'Any chance of some tea?'

Ro could feel the adrenalin pumping round his body. He felt ready for a fight, or a marathon, he was sweating. He glanced down at his tightly clenched fists. He pulled at the orange silicon band around his wrist. Tea. Something normal, that would be good.

'Yeah.'

'Thanks,' the woman said, 'that should be the failsafe nationality test, forget the genetic profiling; tea in a crisis.' She sat down.

Ro grabbed the kettle and shoved the spout under the tap.

'Your kids are Kiran Barry Dylan, aged eight, Maya Bethan Dylan, who's five and Neel Bryn Dylan, who's just two. Is that right?' the man said.

'Yes.'

'Where are they?' the man asked.

Ro did not answer.

'The kids all have middle names beginning with B, that's sweet,' the woman said.

'Yeah, both my wife and I...' he stopped, why would he tell them that Kirsty's second name was Barbara and his was Brendan and they thought it would bind them together for ever?

'Where's your wife?' the man asked.

'She works nights. Can she come?'

'There isn't a form for her. What's her status?'

'English and Welsh. She's VB.'

'You have to choose then. You and the kids go on the railroad or all of you go to London.'

Ro put the teas on the table and sat down.

As late as 2016 multiculturalism had been celebrated. Ro remembered the Sainsbury's Christmas advert: it had featured a happy family, white dad, black mother, a mixed bag of kids. Then Brexit happened and things changed. First, they had chucked out all the Poles, Lithuanians, Romanians, all the East Europeans: everyone who had made the country work. Then they had sent all the Filipinos and European staff in the NHS back wherever. But no one had noticed because they had shut down social security as the national debt spiralled out of control and the NHS went belly-up. The British were not manufacturing and selling enough to trade with anyone and the trade deals post-Brexit were poisonous – when they were made at all. Everyone had to work or starve. There were jobs: all the manual jobs the hard-working immigrants like his dad had done in factories, in the food industry, seasonal field work. Then the nationalism that had emerged with the referendum got people talking about real Britishness. The first indicator of how things were going was in 2018 when there was a scandal about Caribbean Windrush generation being without citizenship – people who had come over as kids were deported when they had no paper trail. From 1948, they had come, along with Asians from India, Pakistan and the far reaches of the obsolete empire. Their great-grandchildren were third and even fourth generation British born; what else could they be? Plans were drawn up for segregation, South African style.

Silicon wristbands were issued; orange for India, green for Pakistan, yellow for the Caribbean, black (how subtle was that) for Africa, on and on it went. Bradford was the first city to be cordoned off, then Luton. Then three years ago, they passed the British Nationality Act. London declared independence. The M25 became the border. London was the only place that a family like his could stay together.

'We'll go to London, all of us.'

'The thing is,' the woman said, 'is to pack. Now. You can work out where you are going while you pack, but if you don't pack Re-Migration Services will be here tomorrow and then you won't have any options.'

'What time does your wife get back?' the man asked.

'Kirsty? Just before six in the morning.'

'We'll send someone to meet her. Meanwhile, can you get ready in thirty minutes?'

Ro stuffed as much clothing as he could into the two jumbo suitcases they had bought for that holiday in 2019. The last time they could afford to go abroad. The last time before their passports had been invalidated. New Year in Lanzarote. They had told the kids that the Christmas present was the holiday and there had been no presents that year. It had been great. Funny, they had thought their previous apartment crummy, but that was before they had lost it; before they had been relocated to this condemned estate. Concrete, high rise and damp. It would be good to leave here but, so far, every change had been for the worse. God, Kirsty was brilliant. How did she find the time to keep the kids cupboards so tidy? The packing was a cinch. He told the kids to fill their backpacks with their favourite toys and books.

'We're going on an adventure', he said.

'Like in the movies?' Kiran said.

'Yeah, adventures always start with packing bags.'

'Can I help?' said Maya.

Passports. Birth certificates. He would need all that. Kirsty kept everything like that in an old biscuit tin in with the saucepans in a cupboard under the kitchen worktop. The tin was from their first Christmas together, she had been pregnant with Kiran and had been craving chocolate like crazy. He had been dead chuffed with the Cadbury's special chocolate biscuit selection. He prised the lid off. All the kids birth certificates were in one plastic folder, the passports in another, along with the deed polls that changed them all from Dhillon to Dylan. He extracted Kirsty's documents and left them in the tin on the kitchen table. She would not trust him to have them. He would see her in the morning.

Minus Six: Tuesday

Steve wished he had not been up late. He was not at his best on four hours' sleep. He took another sip of coffee and shuddered. Maybe three teaspoons of coffee was *de trop* – check that, 'too much'. The Royal Society for the Preservation of English was like a word police force. They were forever calling people out for the misuse and abuse of polluting foreign words and expressions. Adrenalin helped, that's what kept him up late in the first place, the rush of adrenalin from flying dragons and chasing criminals last night.

He stirred in two teaspoons of sugar. Caffeine and pure energy, that's what he needed. He drank it down too quickly to taste it, scanning his emails. He read one twice. Oh, this was going to be fun. A routine pick-up by Re-Migration services had been intercepted, the family (all VNBs) had been warned that they were to be re-migrated but the wife/mother, VB, like a good patriot had told the police. The rendezvous had been intercepted and the family taken into custody. But that wasn't the point; this was an inside job. There would be email trails, CCTV footage, phone calls. This was brilliant. Who needed that coffee?

It was 8:07. He got up and walked towards the boss's office. The commander of BiG Home Security kept his door open, but Steve knew better than to walk in unannounced. He stood at in the doorway and reached in to knock. Commander McPherson looked up from the piece of paper he held pincered between his thumbs and first fingers. The unusual grip was both delicate and crablike.

'Yes?'

'Something's come up!'

'I guessed that. Come in.'

'At 0–600 hours this morning a kidnapping of candidates for Re-Migration was intercepted. The mother of the family alerted us to the planned evasion of Re-Migration.'

'Yes, I am aware of this case. And?'

'Sir, can I undertake a reconnaissance, sorry investigation, into the digital trail?'

'What?'

'They were tipped off, Commander. There has to be a digital trail, it was an inside job.'

The commander sat up straight and looked at him. He had penetrating blue eyes. Steve knew he was meant to feel or understand something, but he could not read McPherson.

'Well, as I had not assigned anyone to the case yet, and since you are volunteering, yes, get on it. And get Norman Marshall in.'

Jenny clicked the mouse to send the email and looked up. In all the cubicles around her everyone was either reading, typing or talking on the phone. A sea of earnest white faces gently bobbing up and down. It had been very different a few years ago. Now everyone was keen they all started work at 8:30. The phone rang. Jenny waited for the third ring before picking it up.

'BVD we aim to please?'

'It's Mark.' He was only in the cubicle two along. He only rang if he could not be seen talking to her.

'Yes,' she kept her voice neutral.

'I just remembered that poet's name.'

'What are you talking about?'

'Dylan B. Thomas.' She had to think; Dylan B? The Dhillons. All those middle names beginning with B. How could her heart jump up her throat like that?

'Oh, yes. He was Welsh. I have to go now.'

She got up and walked past his cubicle. He was still on the phone, talking to a pretend line. She tapped his shoulder and made an elaborate charade about having a fag and went up onto the roof. The affair idea had been a brilliant notion. A few minutes later he joined her. He gave her the stage embrace. They could never risk thinking they were not being watched. He held her close and kissed her hair.

'What happened?' she whispered into his ear.

'The wife would not go when we sent our man to intercept her, we think she must have tipped the police off. They were picked up where they were waiting for her.'

'No way. The kids' own mother?'

'Some people still don't get it. Maybe she thought she could keep the kids and lose their dad.'

'The propaganda is all about immigrants. People just don't think of their own family as immigrants. They think they're immune.'

'Sssh! You're getting too loud.' He started to kiss her again. She clung to him.

'I can't work out if it's a shame or not that you're gay.' She pushed him away and took a long drag of her cigarette.

'Well, I wouldn't necessarily be on your side if I wasn't, would I?'

'True.' The LGBT community had been criminalised again and lost all their civic rights.

'So, what can we do?' Mark said.

'Hope and pray. Hope and pray.'

'I know someone. Let me see.' Mark turned away with a determined look on his face.

The sun was streaming through a crack in the curtains when Norman woke up. It felt late. He rolled over, the sheet on Jenny's side was cold. She was long gone. He had a day off. No rush. It had gone ten by the time he had set off from Ashford. Tess had been very welcoming. They had not made it into the bedroom the first time; he had shagged her on the carpet of the living room. Maybe that is where the word shagpile came from. It had been a rather short tufty acrylic number; his knees were sore from carpet burn. Then she had made him supper, just like that, her work top unbuttoned and her lower half naked. It was just a quick pasta but that had given him the energy to take her again in her bed. She had obviously read *Fifty Shades of Grey* because she had all these manacles and silk ribbons in her bedside cabinet that she had shown him. That was the one dumb thing she had done. People just did not get it; he was a pro, not a sadist. He did what he did for work, not for pleasure. In the circumstances, flipping her over seemed the right tactic. It fed into her fantasy and he got a tight fuck. All in all, a satisfactory outcome. Then he had needed that coffee, before he hit the road; Tess had seemed a bit stiff as she moved around the kitchen making it. Maybe getting her to suck him off while he drank the coffee was a bit too much. The long and the short of it was that it all took a long time and Jenny was tucked up in bed asleep when he got home and she had left for work before he woke up. She must have been a good mood because she had made him pancakes and left them under a plastic microwave cover with a Post-it note: 'Zap for 1–2 minutes, Love you, Jxx'.

After his shower he borrowed some of Jenny's body cream. He sniffed it, a faint floral smell, he could live with that, and rubbed it onto his knees; it stung. He listened to the 9:00 news while he ate the pancakes. They were interviewing the Trade Minister; bloody Londoners were trying to wriggle out of the new food import duties again. Well, we have them over a barrel. It's a city not a farm; they need our farming products. He took his coffee to his desk and turned it on. He scratched his balls, he didn't know when he would next see Tess. Shame. Maybe he could play this whole torturer number to his advantage.

The funny thing was that she had got upset at one point and ranted about the new Tidal Sweep policy. He had seen the encrypted email sent to a closed group in Home Security and Re-Migration: it was a new government directive, the idea being to drop off unwilling VNB re-migrants at sea. They were experimenting for the moment with tides to see where they could safely be disposed of over British waters, expending the least amount of fuel and avoiding the bodies being washed ashore. Tess was upset that two people had been taken from her camp for a test flight. He hadn't had her down as Mother Teresa. It was all the same to him, needs must.

He tapped in his password and smiled as he waited for the boot up to finish. Seventy-two bloody emails in less than forty-eight hours. Some he had seen on his phone yesterday but the last fourteen were from this morning. Three were flagged red and had 'Insider Trading' as the subject. That idiot nerd, Steve, had come up with this heading for any security breach. He might have well just written SECURITY BREACH ALERT.

The van jolted over a bump. Ro opened his eyes, Neel's head bounced on his lap. He cupped the boy's head with his left hand, his other arm stretched around Maya. She had gone to sleep long ago. Kiran was sitting bolt upright opposite, his eyes fixed on him.

'Was that mum in the car? The other car?'

'I think so.'

'Why didn't she come with us?'

'She wasn't allowed.'

The van came to a halt. 9:08. The door on the passenger side opened, then slammed shut. Music from the radio drummed against the partition. After an age the door opened and slammed again, then the same on the driver side. The sound from the radio changed to voices, talk radio. Ro strained to hear the words. If they were talking about the Northern Vote he couldn't tell, 'referendum' was exactly the kind of word that sounded like a roll of thunder reverberating on the partition. The driver door opened and slammed. The van shuddered as the engine started up, mercifully the kids only stirred but did not waken. 9:21. If the North did vote to leave, maybe they could get there somehow. Maybe there would be another place to flee, if he ever got out of the van.

God, he was angry with Kirsty, mad angry, but he did not want to tell Kiran that it was his mum who had turned them in. What had she been thinking? She must have convinced herself that they would deport him and let her keep the kids.

There had been a couple of cases of that reported in the media. Honest citizen rewarded by keeping children. But she could not be that stupid. That was just lies and propaganda. Their only chance of staying together had been going to London. Well, she had blown that. She had lost her children. He'd seen her in the police car. She had tried to get out when they started bundling the kids into the van. A policeman had pushed her back into the car and shut the door. That was last thing he had seen before they had shoved him in. She had chosen to give him up rather than chance it and keep the family together. It was not something he could forgive.

'I want Mummy.'

'I know, I'm sorry, I wish we were all together.'

'Where are we going?'

'I don't know. I'm sure we'll be fine. Maybe they'll bring Mummy afterwards.'

'I want to go home.' Kiran started to cry.

It was going to be another hot day. It was nearly 9:30 and they had finished the field; the team were waiting for the coach to pick them up and take them on to the next. Darcy was filling in forms while the runners were scanning and stacking all the trays. Maisie sat down and pulled the ring off a tepid can of Coke, she took a long drink then opened her bag of crisps. She took turns crunching the crisps in her mouth and sipping the sweet drink. They never normally had to wait for the coach. She closed her eyes.

When she opened them again Darcy was stretched out in front of her sunbathing. She had taken her top off. When she moved, her muscles rippled, not sharp like a man but lean and toned. She was sweating, there was a shine to her back.

The sound of a motor coming around the corner made her look up. It was one of the refrigerated delivery vans. What was that doing here? She closed her eyes again, where was the coach?

'Oy Darcy, wakey wakey. We need to load the van. Special delivery.' Tom's voice broke the lazy quiet. He was walking to the stacks of trays, loaded with the morning's pickings. She always thought he seemed too young to be Harvest Manager. He had pale hazel eyes, short, tidy brown hair and had the lean look of a man who worked out, a lot. He would never look at her the way she looked at him.

'So much for our break,' Maisie said.

'Can't be helped.' Darcy was struggling to pull her bra-top over her head while lying on her front.

'Shall I help?' Maisie started to tug at the elastic with Calvin Klein stamped over it.

'No, I'll be fine.' Darcy rolled over and up and swiftly pulled the top down, not before Maisie caught sight of her breasts; they were smaller than hers, firmer but the nipples, they were long and hard, like nipples that had been sucked. 'Tom's more interested in the trays.'

Darcy looked at her.

Maisie felt a wave of heat flushing over her face. Darcy must think she was gay or bi or something, catching her looking at her tits like that.

'We better get going. Tom looks all flustered.'

Darcy was right. Tom was jumpy. He kept on changing his mind about what to take. He seemed more interested in the size and condition of the packing crates rather than the strawberry selection. He took all the waste berries. He said it was for the transit camp; for once he was not obsessed with quality. They were in the biggest crates. It was not like him at all. And he was right fussy about how they were stacked. He didn't want the truck full, he kept saying it was a special delivery. If Darcy had noticed anything about her looking at her tits she didn't mind or show it. She seemed just as transfixed as Tom in stacking the crates just so.

Norman was on his second circumnavigation looking for a parking space. It was thirty-two minutes since he had read the email relaying Rick McPherson's summons to an emergency meeting. He glanced up at the cellular, concrete Axis building; he had been here when the now defunct British Transport Police had occupied it. There had been a nice leafy car park then. That was before the developers had demolished the car park, before the collapse in property prices when the UK split and the development was moth-balled. Now there were no bloody parking spaces and the Home Security Agency had requisitioned the building. He did not like wearing a suit on his day off, he did not want to get in his car again, and he certainly did not like going into the office on his day off. Nevertheless, thirty-four minutes after the email, he was parking and wondering whether he would have to unbutton his jacket if he ran in it.

Despite his alacrity he was sixteen minutes late when he knocked on the conference room door and walked in.

'Sorry I'm late. I came in as soon as I saw the emails.'

'Good of you, Norman, it's your day off, isn't it?' Rick said. He seemed to be in magnanimous mode. He liked a crisis. Norman reckoned it made him feel powerful. Which he was.

'Duty calls, boss.'

'Steve, can you fill him in?' Rick glanced at Steve, 'Briefly.'

Steve was the idiot nerd who had come up with INSIDER TRADER.

'Yes. Yes. So, we were scheduled to pick up a family of four: Rohan Dylan né Dhillon, Kiran Dylan né Dhill...'

'Spare us the details Steve, just briefly.'

'Yes, ah, a man and his three kids. They were tipped off but the wife is a patriot and she got in touch with us. We intercepted them at their rendezvous spot and we took them into custody. They should be well on their way to the Re-Migration Transit camp by now.'

'Good, Steve, nice and brief.'

'That all seems in hand, boss. Except of course there is the question of the tip off.'

'That's what I thought, Norman, precisely. I'm glad you've come in because I would like you to take on the investigation.'

'Yes, sir, anyone else on it?'

'Just you and Steve. He can back you up with anything you need.'

Steve looked like he was going to come. The idiot boy must have grown up playing games online and now he was doing it for real. Jerk. He had no idea how grimy reality was. Norman shifted in his seat as the memory of Tess's taut back last night crossed his mind.

They waited for the coach to disappear down the mud track. Darcy felt better knowing that no one was watching them anymore. Kelly knew what to do and could lead the team for her until she got back. Tom gave one last look at the interior of the van. All those silent eyes watching them while they had loaded up. It was not the harvest manager's job to deliver produce; nor a team leader's. Produce was always loaded from the pack-house, not straight from the field like this. No one asked why the Transit Camp deliveries were different, why it was always Tom and Darcy in the van. Tom shut the doors and walked round to the front. Darcy got in on the passenger side.

'We've got to keep an eye on Maisie. She's watching me like a hawk.'

'Don't worry, she's too thick to figure it out.'

'Tomasz.' She said quietly as he pulled out onto the country lane that led from the farm down to the main road. She liked the softness of his name, that it didn't seem to end.

'Yes, Darcy.'

'Do you ever get frightened?'

'All the time. All the fucking time. But we have to do these things, don't we?'

'Yes.'

There was not much to say. They knew the routine, they knew what they had to do. She wanted to stretch out her hand and rest it on his thigh. She reached for the console and turned the radio on. NBBC Radio 1 and 2 had British-only policies and there was only so much Merseyside music you could listen to. Even George Michael was off the playlists. She switched to NBBC Radio 4. *Woman's Hour.*

'... *if I understand this correctly, the key to successful jam making is the setting point.*' It was neither Jenni Murray nor Jane Garvey, whose voices she had heard her mother listening to everyday when she was growing up. They had discussed and interviewed women excelling at work, shattering glass ceilings, leading the way, combatting abuse as well as the odd recipe. It was a different story now.

'*Yes, you must be patient, there are no shortcuts, unless you have a jam thermometer of course, other than taking spoonfuls of jam and dropping it on a plate to see if it sets and doing this again and again until it does. You'll know it's right when it forms...*'

Darcy switched it off.

'They can't make their mind up. The place of women is in the home, making jam but, also, they got us all working and off benefits and there's no subsidised childcare anymore. What do they really want?'

'Maybe we should all leave?'

'I don't speak anything but English.'

'I can teach you Polish.'

'Tomasz Lisek,' she said over enunciating it, the way he had taught her, 'I speak it already.'

Cordelia Hughes sat back into the black mesh of the chair. It tilted slightly. The expensive orthopaedic chair and the computer were the only changes she had made to the study. She tapped the faded and scuffed green leather with her indestructible nylon nails. It had been her father's desk and before that her grandfather's and maybe even her great-grandfather's. Everything about the house reeked of tradition, farming, the land and permanence. She was English through and through, even her gene pool was as pristine as you could get. There was a trace of Viking and a hint of Celt, the last significant foreign contribution to her genetic makeup had been from the Normans. She knew this because her interest in breeding extended beyond her strawberry and raspberry farm and horses; a few years ago – before it was mandatory – she had swabbed her mouth with a cotton bud, sent it off in a sterile plastic container and waited for four weeks before receiving by post a package containing her genetic profiling. She should have taken up English Rose growing after that. Her roots could not be deeper, nor her genetic stock purer.

Like every other farmer she knew, she had voted against Brexit. That had just been business sense, she had been worried about her workforce of seasonal labourers. Over the years she had learned a bit of Ukrainian, Polish and Lithuanian when the HOPS scheme had been running, then later Bulgarian and Romanian. She had become friendly with her regular workers; good honest, reliable people. They were polite, respectful and well brought up. Which is more than she could say for the louts that the job-centre had sent her the first year that the SAWS scheme had been suspended. People travelling hundreds of miles because they want to work have a very different work ethic from someone forced to travel ten miles because they have been given no choice.

She opened the spreadsheet to enter the day's figures. She moved her cursor to the second line, under the day's date, and began to type, line by line, typing and pressing enter until she had entered everything. She moved the cursor to 'Data', clicked again on 'Sort', selected 'Team' to sort by. Team Three were again her best pickers. They were kept in separate accommodation, separate transport, separate fields. This daily check was an unnecessary ritual, she knew this would be the result. It was just an unexpected and happy outcome of her decision to break the law.

Over the years many of her pickers had moved on and found permanent jobs in the UK. Overnight they became unwanted.

At first, two years ago, a few, then last year more and now twenty-eight had come back, desperate to work, desperate to stay in the country and pay for their English children's needs. She opened the second drawer on her right, reached in and pulled out an old ledger book. Her father had written 1956 across the front page. She traced her fingers over her father's faded ink lettering. Would he have understood? He had employed only locals. In those days the picking season had only been six weeks' long. Local women had come and stayed, they had run a crèche. In 1964 her father had entered names like Mrs M. Mouse, Mrs C. Miniver, Miss S. O'Hara, Mrs W. Flintstone and Miss B. Boop in the ledger. They would have had been paid cash in hand. That's what had given her the idea.

She leafed through the pages until she found her own entries. 2002 was written across her first page, she turned to July 2004. There were twenty-eight names in the first column: Ewa Trzeboswka, Gosia Wiecanowska, Jacek Żyrtnicki, Marcin Szymczak. In 2004 most of their workers were Polish, some were Latvian, Lithuanian and Slovak. On the screen now, the column for names in Team Three there were twenty-eight other names: Anna Baker, Mary Brown, John Bull, Mark Carpenter... Twenty-eight names. Twenty-eight fictions. Twenty-eight lives.

She found the entry for yesterday. She picked up her father's gold-nibbed fountain pen and wrote down the date, substituting the year 2004 for 2025 and filled in the columns – weight picked, quality, monies owed – taking the figures from the columns on the computer spreadsheet. She had no official record of these people's existence. They were not here. Her crop was picked by twenty-eight ghosts from 2004 and in return she gave them a chance to help their families, a chance to stay. As providence would have it, they picked the most. She closed the cash book and stowed it back in the drawer, then turned off her computer.

She picked up her mobile.

'Any news?'

'Not yet.'

Being an enemy of the state made her nervous. But she was beyond choosing or dropping out. There were too many lives at stake.

Ro nudged the children awake. The van had come to a halt and the engine had been turned off. He could hear voices, the driver and guard he guessed. The voices receded. It was quiet. This must be where they got off. He looked at his watch. 10:20. They had been picked up around 6:00 and been taken to a police station where they spent an hour. They had left there just before 7:00. They could be anywhere. His stomach turned, three hours was enough time to swing round the M25 and out again. Bloody hell, they had probably passed by London. If only they could have gotten out of the van.

Neel was the slowest to wake. Maya rubbed her eyes, while Kiran stared at him with a stony face. The voices moved off.

'I think we've arrived.'

'Where, Daddy?' Maya asked.

'I don't know, sweetheart. Somewhere.'

And then they sat. Five minutes. He knew because he checked his watch many times.

'Daddy, I need to wee.'

'Hello! Anyone there?'

He pulled the door handle. Locked. Silence.

He tried not to look at his watch after he had checked three times while it said 10:29. Time was not passing. There was the rattle of a key on the lock. It didn't turn. Then again.

'Look kids, keep your bags close, real tight. Don't let go of them; it's all we've got.'

The lock turned, and the door opened. A huge man with tattoos on his face opened the door. He was wearing a uniform with short sleeves exposing a lattice work of patterns inked onto his arms. His head was shaven and sat on the thickest neck Ro had ever seen. The man was a muscle bound giant, a veritable skin-head thug.

'Right, grab your bags, leave nothing behind and follow me. Out of here in ten seconds and not a sound from one of you. Got it?' The guard said in a rush.

He reached in and grabbed Neel's bag from his feet.

'Mind, I mean quick.'

'Do as he says, kids.' Ro pushed Kiran and Maya out, handed them their bags and grabbed his bag and Neel's hand. He did not want to mess with the guard. The guard locked the van door.

'Follow me,' he said, pausing as they passed the front of the van to reinsert the keys into the ignition. 'Stay close and not one fucking word.'

'Daddy...' Kiran started.

'Quiet! Don't you speak English?'

The guard moved fast. He took them into a corridor, up a flight of stairs, along past many doors, down, up, along and then down into a dark room. There was nothing in it but boxes. There was a shuttered hatch down one side. They were in a loading bay.

'Sit here,' he pointed at some crates, 'wait and keep quiet. I mean absolutely, not one word, quiet. Don't move 'til that hatch opens and then you go with whoever opens it.' He left, locking the door behind him.

After about forty minutes Tom pulled into Ashford transit camp. Re-Migration? Who were they trying to kid? How could someone born and bred here re-migrate? It made Darcy angry every time she thought about it. The trouble was the news, or the lack of news, all these new words and phrases hid ugly truths just like these billboards painted with pictures of this idyllic vision of England, like Downton Abbey before the First World War. It was all make-believe.

'Food Donation,' Tom told the guard and waved the paperwork at him. The guard took the papers.

'How's it going?' The guard said, still looking down at the papers. He turned the leaves over. Darcy recognised him, he seemed to know them. They came two or three times every week. The guards worked shifts but this one recognised them, she always felt his eyes trailing over her.

'Lots of picking.' Darcy reached over Tom and offered the guard a punnet of strawberries. 'Here, have this.'

'Thanks. Don't see why they should get them all,' he gestured towards the camp. 'In you go.'

The local farmers were all expected to donate to feeding the Re-Migration Transit camp. UNHCR was not giving food to internal refugees and the government said that as unwanted aliens they did not have to provide for them, so all the local farmers were tithed and had to contribute for humanitarian reasons. Tom drove up to the furthest open bay and jumped out. Darcy got out slowly and stretched her arms up. There was a man unloading carrots in the next bay. She waved her arms around in an exaggerated, languorous motion.

'I need a pee,' she said loudly and smiled at the carrot man. She drew out a pack of fags and lit one. She sucked slowly, inhaled and blew out.

'What, you leaving me to unload everything?'

'Yeah,' she winked at the man with his box of carrots.

Tom's phone buzzed. He looked at it.

'Be back in fourteen minutes.'

'You run a tight ship.' She laughed and sauntered off blowing out the smoke. Bay 14, not bad they were at 7. 14 was just round the curve. She counted the numbers painted on the bay doors as she walked along: 8, 9, 10, 11, 12, 13 and 14. There was no one around, no one had followed her. Silence. They had never been wrong so far. She knocked on the shutters.

'Hello. Anyone in there?'

'Yes,' came a man's uncertain voice.

'Listen, mate, we're not playing around. In about ten minutes I'm going to lift this shutter and you and your kids are going to move like the wind and step into the back of my van. This is a rescue. Keep quiet until I come back and get yourselves ready.'

There was silence.

'Did you get that?'

'Yes.'

'Good.'

Ro looked out of the window. He had never seen so much green in his life. Back there in Birmingham they had got out of the city sometimes. They had taken the kids to Warwick

Castle a couple of years ago over Christmas; it had been magic walking round the ruins. When they had climbed up the tower, he remembered Kiran being impressed by the patchwork of bare, muddy fields spread out beneath the grey wintery sky. Now, here in Kent, in July, the sun high in the blue sky, the fields bursting with greenery, the orchards full of pear and apple trees, with miniature hard fruit up amongst the leaves, it made him ache. Tom had said this was the garden of England. It could have been Eden as far as he could tell. But this was it, this was England, this is what it was all about, what made it all tick. He loved it, but it was alien to a city lad, a Brummie like himself.

'Dad!' Kiran called. 'Maya hit Neel.'

'Kids.' He put down the sponge, he would finish washing up later.

Maya and Neel were squabbling. They missed their mum and they did not understand why they had to stay in. It was only Kiran who got it. They were still in danger. They could stay in Tom's house, while a transfer to London was arranged. Then they would begin again.

Maya was sitting on one end of the sofa, Neel on the other, Kiran was jammed in the middle. Maya and Neel were both crying. Tom had no streaming services, only freeview. They were making do with NCBBC and NCBeebies. It was hard to get money for new programming or even the staff. When the BBC had split they had divided up the back catalogue; *In the Night Garden* and *Tweenies* to NBBC, *Teletubbies* and *Go Jetters* to LBC. NBBC showed old programmes back to back. Even a kid could only watch so many repeats without going mad. Tom had a pile of action movie DVDs but they were not kids' fare. He looked at his watch. They had only been here three hours but they were already bored. Tom had told them they had to stay inside until later. The pickers worked on tight shifts. They came back in the early afternoon and it was best to stay indoors until half five when the pickers would be eating dinner, then he could take the kids into the garden. Meanwhile he had to keep them quiet.

Cordelia pushed the keyboard away. She could not concentrate. She fled her office and went out onto the patio. The wind ruffled her hair. It was always windy out here. She loved the lush green fields, the run of trees in the valley lacing the banks of the little river; her favourite view was not enough to calm her. Despite trusting Tom and Darcy, she could not help being jumpy. Nothing was a given in this brave new world. She wanted to talk to them but had to wait until they came back from the fields. People noticed routines and she could not start prowling the poly-tunnels like a hungry leopard, she had to keep to her usual habits. She knew they were back, she had seen the van parked back in the yard, but she wanted to know more. Tomasz was a stickler for security, he would not ring her unless it was vital.

They had never done this before, brought people back, but the railroad had never failed before either. Tom had texted: 'distributor failed to show, still have merchandise'. Keith Vicars had been insistent, if anything went awry she should not ring. Wait to be contacted. She hated waiting.

At 3:00 she made tea and stared out of the kitchen window at the pear trees in the orchard. Her phone sat on the black marble worktop; the screen stayed black, the blue light flashed but it did not ring. She checked for messages, knowing that none had come. The sound of a low wind chime would have announced a message coming in. At eighteen minutes past three she considered the iridescent film that had settled on her untouched tea; scum, chalk from the Kent Weald. She had given up using the water filter to screen out the calcium when she had started taking calcium supplements. A coherent strategy was always the best. She picked up the mug and downed the drink in one go. She grabbed her keys and phone. Time for her round. Habit, the usual, act normal. It was like a mantra.

She drove to the packing shed where all the fruit was stored, labelled, boxed and eventually loaded. She checked the daily figures and exchanged pleasantries in the office, then glanced through the window over the busy machines. Time to check the fields.

Tom was fiddling with a hose when she found him.

'Was it a good day?' she said loudly; the podgy Thanet girl was hanging around as usual.

'We did more than yesterday.' Tom said.

'It's Marcy, isn't it?'

'Maisie.'

'Sorry Maisie, how are you finding the work?'

'The work's fine, I get back ache. But I'm not complaining, I kind of like working outdoors.'

'Oh, you've never done farm work before.'

'Done tomatoes over the winter, and asparagus last year. The Work Task Force sent me. If I hadn't taken it I'd've lost my benefits and child support.'

'How many children do you have?'

'Three, well two now.'

'Well, you must miss them.'

'Yeah, I've got my day off Friday.'

'Oh, have a good day. I'm sorry, I shouldn't keep you, you need to go and rest.'

'Yeah, thanks.'

Maisie left. Cordelia waited until she was out of hearing range.

'So, what happened?'

'The pick-up was fine. Everything went well. The cargo was in the right bay. But when we drove to our drop-off point, the other lot didn't show up. We waited twenty minutes as per the rules and then I brought them here. I've put them in my house.'

'That's not good.'

'I know, but what else could I do? I've told them to stay indoors.'

Darcy joined them.

'I've just been round to the house. I gave them some books I'd bought for Alfie.'

'That was kind.'

Cordelia had not noticed it before, but it was suddenly evident. Tom and Darcy were standing just a bit too close. Maybe they did not know it yet, maybe they did, but something was happening between them.

'No, it was obvious. I can always buy new ones.' Darcy looked tired. 'I'm off now, I want to get home for a few hours.'

'I'll drive you. Tom, you can pick her up later, can't you?' There was nothing wrong with shooting cupid's arrow.

Darcy watched as Cordelia made a U-turn then drove back down the way they had come. Cordelia knew how much she missed

Alfie, she was a good woman. She opened the wooden gate in the stone wall that marked the original boundary of Cordelia's estate. The pebble track, edged on either side by overgrown hedges, led home. They lived in an old gamekeeper's cottage, a few hundred yards up, invisible from the road. She took a deep breath and started walking fast.

It was always the same. Every time she had managed to come back, the excitement was almost painful. It was early, not even four. She would have a few hours with him. The thought of his wet kiss made her stomach flip.

She rang the bell as she slid the key into the lock. It was hard to come back every day during the harvest, it felt almost rude not to announce her arrival. The smell of onions hit her nose; she headed straight into the kitchen. Her mum was standing stirring the onions in a pan,

'Hi, nice surprise, Love. He's in the garden.'

She gave her mum a kiss. Potatoes were boiling in a pan.

'Shepherd's pie, my lucky night. Is there enough for me?'

'And more.'

'Mind if I invite a friend?'

She stepped out of the kitchen and looked down the garden. She couldn't see him but she knew where he was. But first she had to send a text: 'If you want to meet Alfie, come for shepherd's pie at six.'

She ran as fast she could down the hill. The cottage was small, but the most important thing was that the garden was totally secluded. The lawn was on a hill and it dived down into a dell merging with a woodland. A small stream trickled past as the bottom and she knew that's where Alfie would be playing with the water. He was only four but he had had to grow up fast. He could look after himself.

He must have heard her because he was running up the hill towards her.

'Mummy! Mummy!' He flew into her arms and she span him round, laughing.

'Oh, I've missed you so much.'

He clung to her like he would never let go.

Ro opened the kitchen door into the garden. The air was thick and warm and smelt of, he didn't know, he had never smelt anything as heavy and sweet. All those air-fresheners that Kirsty bought to cover up the damp stench, none of them ever smelt like this. Tom had said that after 5:30 it was safe to go out. All the pickers would either be in the showers or hanging out together. He took a step out, it was quiet, no one was around. There was a wall of trees around the left-side and end of the garden, the lawn was bordered with flowers and a thick spread of shrubs. Halfway along the right-hand side, a path led through the floral border and bushes into a small grove of apple, pear and cherry trees rustling in wind. There were so many different greens. If he had not felt scared and angry, this could have been a holiday cottage.

'OK, kids, we're going to play silent hide and seek again. And I mean it, not a word. Whoever makes a sound goes straight back in the house.'

He had hit upon the idea earlier in the afternoon, impressing on them the need to stay quiet.

'Neel can't keep quiet,' Kiran said.

'I can.'

'Look, I really mean it. No second chances. One sound and you're back in.'

They took turns being It, hiding and spying and racing back to the biggest pear tree in the orchard which was home, but if anyone made a noise they were out and had to go back in. It was hard to spot their dark skins in the mottled shade; for once their skin colour was an advantage. There had been a lot of sulking earlier, but after their house-bound practice games they were like silent and deadly ninja, delighted by their stealth and ability to stay quiet. Neel was the only one who still gave away his position by suppressed snorting as you walked past.

Kiran was It when Ro saw the woman coming around the side of the house. Maya and Neel were hiding behind the shrubs in the border, Ro was standing behind an azalea bush. The woman was short, her dark hair tied in a ponytail, tight leggings, a short sky-blue top too tight over her breasts. He could not see her face, she was intent on staring through the windows as she walked round the house. Where was Kiran? He must have finished counting by now. The woman stood, her face pressed close against the window; he would see smear marks from her sweat later when he looked out of the same pane. He heard a rustle, Kiran came up behind him.

'Who is she?' Kiran said, his voice barely audible.

'I don't know. It's not Darcy. That's for sure.'

It was just before six when Darcy heard a car turn off the main road and rumble up the stony lane. She was reading Alfie a story in the front room. He looked up from the pictures.

'Is Auntie Cordelia coming?' Alfie asked.

'No', she kissed her the top of his head, 'it's Tom.'

She got up to peer through the window. Tom was walking from his car. He had put on a white shirt and what looked like a new pair of jeans. She had never seen him in a shirt before. He looked good.

'Come on, Alfie, let's go and open the door for Tom.'

She opened the door as Tom stepped onto the old flagstone front step. She could feel the grin stretching over her face.

'Who's Tom?' Alfie said, behind her.

'I'm your mummy's friend,' said Tom, dropping down to squat, 'and you must be Alfie. It's good to meet you finally.' He took Alfie's little brown hand and clasped it in his pale, Polish one, giving a gentle shake.

Darcy's mum acted as if it was completely normal to have guests to tea. In truth, Tom was the first visitor they'd had other than Cordelia since they moved here. No one came, no one could come, no one could see Alfie. But her mum did not give any hint of that. When they had all eaten, Tom came up with her and sat at the end of the bed watching her read stories to Alfie.

'Good night, Alfie,' Tom said. 'It was good to meet you.'

'Night, night, Tom.' Alfie said sleepily. 'Mummy, stay.'

'I'll wait for you,' Tom said and slipped out of the room.

Darcy loved lying on the bed with Alfie moulded against her. Usually she stared entranced as his face relaxed, as he fell into his world of dreams. Today, it was different, she was straining to hear where Tom was. She could hear her mum tidying up downstairs; the radio was on, there was no other sound. She closed her eyes and listened and waited until Alfie's breathing slowed and fell into a deep, quiet and regular pattern. Slowly she unwound her arms from him and slid off the bed, careful not to wake him.

She closed his door. The TV was on downstairs now, her mother must have finished in the kitchen. If Tom were downstairs she would be talking to him, a visitor was too rare a treat for her to ignore him. She turned away from the stairs. Her bedroom door was ajar, she pushed it open. Tom was lying on her bed asleep.

She sat down on the edge of the bed. His face looked as pliable and tranquil as Alfie's.

'Tomasz.'

He opened his eyes.

'Alfie is a lovely boy,' he said after a long moment.

'Thanks.'

His hand reached up to caress her face. She closed her eyes; finally. She turned her face into his hand and kissed his palm. His hand fell away, she bent towards him as he strained up, his lips were as soft as she had imagined.

'You know that I'm in love with you?' he said when they broke off to breathe.

'Good, that makes us even.'

His shirt must have been new; the buttons resisted her pushing them through the stiff material.

No one was in her hut when Maisie got back. She was glad that Jane and Amy were not there. She felt out of sorts. They kept to themselves. They weren't unfriendly, they just weren't interested. She had gone for a walk after she had left Tom's house but still felt confused. She got on her bed and looked up at the wooden slats supporting Darcy's mattress. Darcy had the top bunk, she clambered up more easily than she could. Maisie stroked the photos of the children that she had clamped into place with the slats. She missed them. She had her shower, sat on her bunk and tried not to ring home. It was expensive. Bleedin' hell, Mum was totally capable of taking the kids to the beach and getting them home. So what if they fell over, so what if they got wet? Her mum knew the tides. She wouldn't let them get swept away. She was not an idiot. But, as Maisie sat up in bed, the gnawing anxiety was too much; she had to get out. Stiff and sore as she was, she had to walk. She went to the toilets. She had always been carefree until she had lost Jayde. Things were different now. Jane and Amy were getting into their bunks when she got back.

'Evening.'

'G'night,' they said in unison.

Two hours later she was still reading news on her phone. There was a Twitter storm over who would be the first person to be hanged. People were fighting over whether it should be a VB or VNB. It was sick, hanging was from the dark ages. Everyone knew that.

'You still awake?' Darcy said when she came back into the hut. Amy and Jane slept through quiet conversations.

'Yeah, my mum's been texting; she and the kids are all right.'

'How many you got?'

'Three. Two.'

Darcy stared at her. A strange look flashed over her face.

'You live with your Mum?'

'Yeah, it's worked out. Used to have my own council flat, benefits and everything. Life was good, the kids' fathers would help out, well at least Jay did, even with the other two but then, you know.'

'I know.'

'You were too young to vote.'

'Don't I know it.'

'We had no idea, Darcy. We had no idea.'

'So then, before we left, you could afford to live alone with the kids.'

'You know what, it was all right but it is nice living with my mum. I just wish I didn't have to work away.'

'Or work at all?'

'I dunno, the work is not bad. I just get anxious. I need to see them.'

'Yeah,' Darcy said quietly, Maisie wasn't quite sure she had spoken. She was looking out the door. 'It's gone ten. Lights out?'

'Sure.'

Minus Five: Wednesday

Ro could not sleep. He had tried. The kids were sharing the double bed in the spare room. He had tried kipping on Tom's sofa. He had watched TV most of the night, dozing between bad movies. Tom had come in just after ten last night and gone straight up. The last twenty-four hours had been insane. It was the stuff of movies. He was exhausted, but every time he shut his eyes the horror of the agents pulling them from the van, the kids screaming and the look on Kirsty's face woke him back up. She had betrayed them. She was deluded. And where did she think they would be sent? His dad had come from somewhere near Amritsar and had been brought up a Sikh. But he had dropped all that when he had met Ro's Irish-Brummie mum. Where would they send him? Home? The only home he knew was Birmingham, the only language he spoke was the King's own, and he was no more Indian than Irish. He had not been in a *gurdwara* even half a dozen times. His dad never wore a turban. As for his mum, she had dragged him to family weddings and christenings in St Chad's but not much more. Villa Park was his temple, Aston Villa his tribe.

The floorboards above creaked. It was half past four. Not even twenty-four hours since they had been nabbed. Tom was up; the kids were on the other side. Ro got up and filled the kettle.

'I made you a tea,' Ro said as Tom came into the kitchen, 'I wasn't sure what you eat.'

'Thanks, not to worry.' Tom opened the fridge, grabbed the

loaf – Ro had never seen bread like it, heavy and dense with a sour smell – and some cheese.

Ro settled down on the other side of the table. He sipped his tea, waiting for Tom to sit down.

'We really appreciate this.'

'You don't have to thank me. Do someone else a favour down the line.'

'Yeah. I will.'

Tom spread mustard on the cheese then took a bite.

'This woman came snooping round the house yesterday afternoon.'

'What?'

'I was out in the garden with the kids when she just turned up and started staring through the windows. She didn't see us, luckily we were playing hide and seek.'

'What did she look like?'

'Short, plump, her leggings and top were a bit too small, her hair was pulled back really tight in a pony-tail.'

'Maisie.'

'The weird thing was that after she had stared through the window, she sat down against the wall and bawled like a child for about a minute. Then she just got up and went off. We waited about ten minutes before heading back into the house. I kept the curtains drawn after that.'

'That's odd.'

'Who is she?'

'She works with Darcy. She must have seen Darcy heading down this way. I asked her to check my messages on my other phone before she went off. I have a phone I use for this stuff, I keep it hidden in one of the outhouses here. Maisie must have followed her.'

Tom got up and walked round the kitchen and the other rooms.

'What do you reckon she saw?'

'She had a good look through the living room window. The only give away would have been the kids' books and if she were particular I guess she could have counted the plates on the drying rack from lunch in the kitchen.'

'She's not too bright, the plates would have meant nothing, but the books. She'll wonder.'

'And like I said, she sat down and had a good old cry. It was weird.'

'Maybe she misses her kids.'

'Yeah, but why would she follow Darcy?'

'Don't know, but sometimes I think she might like her.'

'*Like* like her?'

Cordelia hated networking and hated small talk and yet here she was at the local branch of the National Farmers' Union discussing the weather with people she did not care for. The venue at least was nice, she walked over to the window and looked out at the view. Lord Lopcombe had spent his money well. The family who had lived here before, for generations, had to sell fast when they lost their wealth, good investments turned bad overnight after the country left the EU then split. The park was gorgeous; it must be Capability Brown.

'Admiring the view?'

Cordelia turned to see Lord Lopcombe offering a glass of champagne to her.

'Yes,' she took the glass, 'thank you.' She took a sip. 'Yours?'

She had not drunk any champagne for at least two years, but this Kentish sparkling wine was rather good. It would be tempting to keep downing it but she had to stay alert. 'What grapes do you use?'

'Oh, chardonnay, pinot noir and pinot meunier, I believe.'

'It tastes like the real thing.'

'Don't say that. We've trademarked the name *Bubbly*. It is the real thing. With the hike in temperatures we've had, we have perfect conditions here now.'

'Champagne by another name.'

'Ms Hughes, may I remind you that Bubbly is the real British thing.'

'Quite so. Cheers. To the "Best of British".'

Cordelia took a long sip. It was as good as any champagne because the grapes had been planted by Taittinger, the French champagne firm, before they had been forced to sell as part of the 'Buy Back British' campaign. Cordelia knew that Lord Lopcombe of Chilham, formerly Steve Lopcombe, a corporate asset stripper, had purchased the estate at a rock-bottom price but knew nothing about wine-making, the soil, the grapes, the harvest. As the market went into freefall when foreign companies were forced to sell, Lopcombe was one of many City boys and girls who grew fat on the fire sales. None of which stopped him from being the chairman of the local branch of the NFU.

'How's this year's crop?'

'We've had plenty of sun, that has to be a good thing.'

She let the lord slip away and he beelined a younger, blonde woman: Sandy Fotherhill. Or was that Melsom? She could not remember if the third marriage had taken place or not. Sandy was one of those women who took a professional approach to hypergamy, marrying up. Cordelia put her glass down and leaned back against the book case. She was a longstanding member of the Kent NFU, and she knew everyone there, but the one person she wanted to see was absent: Keith Vicars.

Keeping track of all the people, their politics, their sympathies was not second nature to Cordelia but she had learned, over the last few years, that if she was to be amongst those fit enough to survive, it was as important to observe people's behaviour as the traits of her strawberry varieties. How things developed, what opportunities presented themselves, what avenues were dead ends, this all came down to people. She would never have been interested in Sandy before. It *was* Melsom now, she remembered, the wedding photos had been in the *Birmingham Times*. She hated the paper but made herself read it, it was the only national broadsheet now – Murdoch had bought the *Birmingham Mail* and merged it with *The Times*. She knew Sandy from the social life page. She was a woman who had not only made a career out of marriage but she was a superb operator. Her husbands were successively more wealthy and powerful, and each one was better connected. The new Mrs Melsom was wearing a string of large white pearls, almost the size of the green raspberry buds on the canes under Poly-tunnel 12 right now, that shimmered as they moved slowly over her neckline. It was low enough to offer hope of seeing more, but above her cleavage. The way she was smiling and laughing with the boring Lopcombe was impressive. The woman was a consummate performer.

Where was Keith? She needed him, she needed help with the transport to London. She surveyed the room again, refused another tall-stemmed glass of not-Champagne and waited. Mrs Melsom had extracted herself from Lord Lopcombe's admiration and walked across the room greeting everyone with a smile and an exchange of words.

'Hello, I'm Sandy Melsom, I don't think we've been formally introduced, but you look like the only other intelligent being in this room.'

'Cordelia Hughes.'

'I know. I just needed to let you know that Keith Vicars won't be coming; he is – how should I put it? – having talks. ' She smiled sweetly at Cordelia.

'I...' Cordelia fell silent. Having talks? He was being interrogated.

'How lovely to have met you,' Sandy Melsom turned and walked away.

He had been caught. Would he give them away? Cordelia made herself go and talk to the tomato growers clumped in a huddle. She discussed this year's sunshine, drip hydration and hydroponics, climate change, the scarcity of good labour and on and on, moving from group to group so that she could keep an eye on Sandy Melsom.

As interrogation rooms went this was satisfactory. There was a table, two chairs facing each other either side, another plastic one by the door for the guard he had just sent out and a camera fixed to the wall. Norman could not see the usual tiny green light, but you could not tell these days if it was active or not. Technology had moved on. Norman was happy. He was a pro and he liked to do things right. He did not often have that pleasure. The man in front of him was tall, well-built, probably a rugby player in his time and he had the erect posture that just had soldier stamped all over him. This would be good.

'Mr Vicars, I understand that the police believe that you are responsible for the movement of illegally trafficked persons.'

'That would be a crime.'

'A capital crime.'

'Really?'

'For the purposes of the Death Penalty Act, trafficking and sabotaging Re-Migration are classed with treason which, as I am sure you know, along with espionage, murder and paedophilia, are all capital crimes.'

'I have never broken the law. I swore allegiance to the crown.'

'And which crown would that be?'

Norman liked this game. There were of course two crowns. King Harry ruled in London and King William in Windsor. The Queen had died as her united kingdom tore itself apart. Charles declared himself the defender of faiths and had surprised everyone by staying in London when it ceded. He'd died on the job though. Now they had Harry with his Black American wife, Meghan. William and Kate, surprised everyone else by moving out of London and taking up residence in Windsor.

'King William! Is there another?' Vicars stared at him. His face a mask. 'I've seen you before.' Vicars said in a matter of fact voice.

'I doubt that.'

'In Helmand. 2009. Operation Panther's Claw.'

He could feel Vicar's eyes drilling through him.

'You were in the Mercians.'

Norman felt his face flush.

'You can't remember me?'

The interview was not going how Norman had expected. 'This is irrelevant, Mr Vicars.'

'Lieutenant Colonel Vicars.'

Norman tried to resist it but he felt his body stiffening and rising to attention even though he was sitting down. They had met, he remembered the voice now. In a tent. Late one night. Bloody hell. He had been one of the Light Dragoons.

'Staff Sergeant Marshall? I remember; I thought it would have been funny if you had got to the top. Field Marshal Marshall.'

Norman liked to be in control. He liked things to follow the plan.

'Don't you remember me?'

'You were there on 2nd July.'

Vicars smiled. '2009 seems a long time ago. We knew who the enemy was there, didn't we?'

Norman gaped at him. His head was swimming. He had been called in to investigate a man the Kent Police suspected of trafficking people from Kent into London. The man in front of him was a veritable war hero. He remembered him in action that night when Operation Panther's Claw had started; the Mercians and the Light Dragoons had collaborated with the Danish Battle Group north of Lashkar Gah, part of a massive multi-national push against the Taliban in Helmand. He had seen Vicars in action: decisive, informed, fearless; in short, commanding. The best kind of officer.

Back in the bloody tunnels again. The day was dragging, probably because it was baking hot. Maisie tugged at the strawberry, it did not want to come off. She pulled harder than she should and felt it squashing between her fingers.

'Fuck.'

'What's up?' Darcy peered through the leafy bush from the other side of the table. She must have started working that aisle after her or just sprung from nowhere.

'Fucking strawberries. I never thought you could hate them.'

Darcy paused and looked at her, her fingers momentarily frozen, grasping a berry lying on the wide band tape that supported the dangling trusses of fruit. Then her fingers moved, seeming to pluck and drop the berries into the box automatically. Maisie squeezed until there was a red mess between her fingers. She threw it as far as she could. It hit the tunnel wall, leaving a red smudge.

'Is everything all right?'

'I'm fine.'

'Something's bugging you.' Darcy was ahead of her already, moving down the table, berry after berry, each plucked with care and laid down with precision.

Maisie shrugged, there was no real reason for being annoyed but she was. 'I dunno.'

'Well, it's got to be home or here.'

'Like I said the kids are fine; my mum is fine.'

'So, it's here.'

'I guess so,' Maisie lifted the leaves of the bush in front of her, there were two berries this side.

'They docked your wages?'

'No, nothing like that.'

'Is Tom being an arse again?'

'No, well yes.'

'What do you mean?'

'I think that he likes you, like more than you think, I'm worried for you.'

Darcy's hands hesitated then resumed their flow. 'You don't need to worry about me. And like I said his bark is worse than his bite.'

'I guess but be careful.'

'Thanks,' Darcy said then turned to shunt her trolley further down the aisle.

Maisie could not tell her, she would think she was weird. But yesterday afternoon, just when she left Darcy with Tom and Mrs Hughes, she had waited outside to see if Tom would hassle her. Mrs Hughes had left them then Tom had said something to Darcy. Then Darcy had started off down the path that led to Tom's place. He was the only one not in the dorms, he had his own cottage, probably a game keeper's or something once, now it was off down a track on its own. Darcy had headed off and disappeared round the bend and Tom had just stayed for a while watching her go. She could not say why but as soon as he had gone she followed Darcy down the path. The strange thing was Darcy didn't seem to be there. She knew because she had looked in every bleedin' window in the house. She didn't even know why she had done that, but she had seen no trace of Darcy. The odd thing was there was a pile of kids' picture books on the living room floor. She had no idea that Tom had a family. It was odd. Still didn't explain why she was pissed off.

Norman did not slouch, he was proud of his military bearing, but he was inclined as much as his rigid office chair allowed. He hated this part of the job; desk work. He clicked on the double back arrows, then play. He was missing something. Steve had sourced all available security videos from the van's route. It had stopped only once at a motorway service station. The CCTV footage from the pumps, the shops and the toilets showed the guard getting out and filling up, getting some snacks, and going to the loos, then the driver took his turn. The rear of the van was not opened. They didn't take another break. He played the tracking record of the trip back carefully. Ashford gate log showed they arrived at 10:18. The CCTV showed them driving around the outer-ring into a loading bay. There was no camera inside the bay itself. At 10:21 they emerged into the main office. They were not in hurry, grabbed coffees from the machine, chatted to other guards and eventually signed in and handed over the papers for the family at 10:28, which matched the register. They left the office at 10:32 and were back reporting the van's mysterious loss of its cargo at 10:39. They had searched for seven minutes before reporting back. Was that the time they had used for getting a story together? A whole family, a man and three kids, they could not just vanish. And the van was locked when the driver got back. The family did not show up on any of the internal cameras. Whoever got them out knew where the cameras were. Steve had checked all the other vans going in and out that day.

On paper he had been certain that Vicars was involved but he had let him go. Evidence was one thing but he believed in following his instincts and his instinct told him that a soldier like Vicars didn't do betrayal. You stay in line, take orders, give orders, but you don't change sides. It was ingrained in him, he knew what it felt like. Rule Britannia and all that. The man could no more betray Britain than he could pretend to be a civvy.

But then who could have done it? He had gone through the log book that day, he had checked all the CCTV footage, there was nothing, everyone, every vehicle that had gone in and out that day was as usual. Medical supplies, food supplies, the local tithed product drop offs, even strawberries – those re-migrants had nothing to complain about. There had been nothing exceptional, nothing untoward.

The keys. He checked the logs again and the driver's interview. He said the van was locked but he never mentioned the keys. He picked up the phone and rang the Re-Migration Services Transit Department.

'Can I speak to Simon Iverson please.'

He waited.

'Who wants to talk to me?' A gruff voice sounded out of the phone.

'Norman Marshall here, BiG Home Security Agent.'

'Sorry Mr Marshall, I didn't know it was you.' He liked it when the tone changed like that, just short of obsequious.

'Not a problem, Simon, just one more question: where were the keys?'

There was a silence. Norman knew to wait.

'In the ignition. I left them in the ignition. They were still in the ignition when I got back. The van was still shut.'

'You might want to think about why you did not volunteer this information when you submitted your report, or when you spoke to me.'

'I fucked up, didn't I?'

'That's the best interpretation. Goodbye, Mr Iverson.'

Norman ended the call and dialled the Home Security Desk Sergeant.

'Arrest Simon Iverson at Re-Migration Services and hold him

for questioning. Perverting the course of justice, aiding and abetting criminal acts.'

Maisie was hiding in Tom's garden. She was not even sure why she was doing it. It was the kids' books on the floor. That had spooked her, she was not sure why. Well, it was to protect Darcy, wasn't it? Darcy was her friend and she didn't want her getting mixed up with a man with a past, a man with kids. She knew about guys like that: they told you they loved you, had their way with you and then they were off to the next conquest. Well, Jay had not been all bad, he had at least helped out with the other kids. But if she had never met Jay, she'd never have had Jayde, and she would never have had this pain now. Fuck Jay, fuck them all. She didn't want Darcy getting hurt like that.

She had come down here as soon as their shift was over. She knew that Darcy would report back to Tom, she seemed to spend more time going over the crop numbers with him every day. Then Mrs Hughes would wander down from the big house and they would have their little confab. Yeah, people had routines, did everything like clockwork, it made it dead easy to spy on them. She thought she would come down here and see what's what. The strange thing was that she could not peek in downstairs like the day before, the curtains were drawn now.

She sat down. She could wait a long time. Anyone used to Thanet bus services could wait. Although a bench in a bus shelter would have been better than the dried brown mess of old flowers under this bush. The wait was shorter than she had thought. She heard them laughing first. They were coming down the lane. Tom and Darcy. Then the weird thing was they went down the side of the house, stopped there and then went all silent. She levered herself onto all fours and crawled through the bush, staying low trying not to make a noise, watching out for crackly leaves until she could see better. The sounds were clearer now, Darcy was gasping, and Tom grunting, he had her shoved up against the brick wall as he thrust his way into her again and again. Darcy's hands were splayed on his bum, pulling him in. Then she had her hands around his face, like she could not keep her hands off him. The poor thing was lost.

Thank the fuck, it didn't take long. It was pathetic the way they just clung to each other when it was done. Then they were rearranging their clothes, laughing, murmuring and one more kiss like they didn't want to stop. The bit she did not get was why have a fuck outside if you lived alone. Duh! He didn't, that was it. There were kids inside.

Jenny sipped the wine. It was a good thing she liked dry whites. She turned the bottle around, this one was called Kent Maide, the last bottle she had tried had been Boudicca. French wine was just too expensive these days, she did not even look at the bottles from Down Under. This was her favourite part of the day; she came home, rang her mum, cooked, ate and then put her feet up with a glass of cold white wine in front of the TV. If it weren't for the news she could pretend that everything was all right. The phone rang. Jenny pointed the remote at the TV and paused the news. The screen froze on an image of a traffic queue. Some Northern separatists had tried to blow up the Humber Bridge. The terrorists had killed themselves and made a small dent in the road surface. The resulting obstruction had

caused a 'major inconvenience' according to the newsreader.
She picked up the phone.

'Hi, love,' Norman said.

'Where are you? I was famished, so I ate without you.'

'Sorry, I've just got this lead that I have to follow.'

'I thought you'd be home by now if it was just office work.'

'Yeah, I might have to head back to Ashford.'

That wasn't good, she did not want him sniffing around
there.

'Oh, Norm, not tonight. I was looking forward to a movie, a
bottle of wine and you know, you.'

'I guess it can wait 'til tomorrow.'

'Good. Hurry on home, I'll be waiting.'

'On my way.'

She poured her wine down the sink. What a waste, but
she needed her wits about her. She walked into the bedroom,
pulled off her sweat pants and top, opened her drawers and slid
her lacy satin nightdress out from underneath a pile of neatly
folded pyjamas. She put his favourite single malt whisky on
the table with a glass and found space for another wine in the
fridge. She had to keep him sweet, she needed to know how
his investigation was going, best to get him pissed. There was
a time when she had been love-struck by him, he was such a
man's man; taciturn, reliable, good with his hands, just really
solid, but she had not understood until now how inflexible he
was. He could not adapt: for King and Country, that's all he
believed in. Even if the country ain't no more and there were
two Kings to choose from.

Even though she knew that Mark could never really be interested in her, she wondered what he saw when he kissed her?
The mirror showed her a well-kept woman in her forties. It was

better to have smiled her way into having crows' feet around her eyes than to have earned frown marks. Her skin was still soft if not as taut as before. Her smoker friends all had leathery skin by now. She had kept her figure; she had not fluctuated more than 2lbs either side of her wedding weight. And never having breastfed her tits were in good shape too. Not bad. She slipped the nightie on and then tugged it forwards, exposing her cleavage. Mark at least saw her, whereas Norman's eyes always seemed distant. She guessed that he was thinking about his other women when he was with her. Yet there was some vestige of his love for her still in there, he did still come back every time, and he still liked to make sure she was his. It was the one thing that had always worked for them. She picked up the lipstick, a touch of red, a flushed look never hurt. She rubbed her finger over the lipstick and then smeared it over her lips. She could feel her lips tingling. She did not need to pretend.

Sometimes she hated him, sometimes she thought she had a crush on Mark, and then other times, like now she wanted to have his arms round her, to have him pummelling her and calling her name even though she knew he was a menace to society, a fascist shit. Maybe it was his certainty that was so attractive.

'You solved the case already?' she said an hour or so later.

He was absent-mindedly playing with her nipples, she was still astride him, she liked to feel him diminish inside.

'No, not quite.'

'Well, I think I got a lead.'

'Oh,' she leaned forward, dangling her breasts over his face. If she kept him distracted he was more likely to blab.

'You trying to wear me out?'

'Just making up for a bit of neglect.' He sucked hard, she pulled away. 'So what lead?'

'Oh, it had to be an inside job, in Ashford.'

She reached behind and grabbed his balls. 'An inside job you say.'

'Yeah, someone who knew when they would arrive, and knew how to get them out. One of the security guards would be my guess.'

Minus Four: Thursday

The bathroom was Maisie's least favourite place. If you got up really early you could have a long unhurried wash, but then you would be knackered all day. If you left it late you could get in without a wait but have only a few minutes in the shower. Mostly the cubicles would all be full and there would already be a queue. Maisie shuffled forwards. Only one more person ahead of her for the shower. She had not woken up early enough. She had felt all riled and had not slept well. Still she just had to get through today and she'd be home tonight. She leaned against the wall and closed her eyes, someone had put the NBBC news on.

'...*the Northern terrorists are in the sights of the police. The Home Secretary announced in Birmingham that no more terrorist acts would be tolerated,*' the newsreader said.

Where was the Humber Bridge anyway? She didn't see how that affected her. She returned her attention to the news.

'... *alert. The Kent police force announced the kidnapping of a family in safe keeping. Rohan Dylan and his three children were taken from the authorities by...*'

Darcy spilled out of the shower cubicle.

'Why are we listening to this miserable crap?' Darcy said as she reached for the radio. Her towel fell, her body glistened, drops of water shimmered over her toned flesh. She put the radio down.

'There that's better.'

The sound of staccato plucked guitar strings bounced off the tiles. Darcy bent over to pick up her towel moving to the rhythm of the music. Maisie stepped closer. She was next in line now. Why couldn't she take her eyes off Darcy's arse? The same arse that Tom was shafting. Bloody hell, why could she not stop looking at her?

'Heh, heh, heeeeh,' Darcy sang along.

'What we got to listen to you singing now?'

'Oh, Maisie, it's fun.' Darcy danced, her hips gyrating, one arm moving as the other clutched the towel. She flashed Maisie a smile then continued singing.

'Why don't you join in,' she danced over to the mirrors, 'It's good exercise anyway.'

A shower door opened. It was her turn; Maisie stepped into the shower.

It was just gone 10:02, Jenny's fresh cup of coffee was steaming in her chipped mug and she had pressed pause on the BiG news feed that flashed onto her screen on the hour. Keeping up with the news was compulsory for any government employment. Being informed was a good thing in a functioning democracy but being force fed propaganda was another thing. She had frozen the screen on the face of Kirsty Dylan. She dreaded the news but she had to watch; her computer would be locked until she had finished. She clicked on the continue arrow. Somewhere, someone or something had logged her pausing.

'*...not much to ask. I don't know how anyone could do this, I just want my kids to be safe and sound.*'

You could read between those lines. Was she talking about their 'kidnapping' or their rendition by the state. Either way the woman looked an emotional disaster. Someone should have got her to brush her hair or wipe the mascara. Or maybe they had, maybe they had back-combed her hair and smudged the mascara. Nothing could be taken at face value these days. Certainly not the news. The newsreader was interviewing a psychologist now.

'... *children of this age will be traumatised. Taken from a secure setting to uncertainty...*'

The screen showed photos of the children Kiran, Maya and Neel. Their ages flashed up below their names, their faces open and smiling. God, they must have taken the flat apart to get all those photos so quickly.

Jenny got up as soon as the bulletin was finished.

'Coffee break?' she asked Mark, holding her mug aloft for everyone to see. Was that a double bluff or just a bluff?

It was blustery on the roof top. Mark held her in his arms. They had kissed as per their roles. Her heart was thumping hard, she was sure he could feel it.

'You're worried?' he whispered into her ear.

'Norman knows it was an inside job in Ashford.'

'That is kind of obvious.'

'He interviewed a guy, some army bloke. He let him go, soldiers' code of honour or something, but I think he'll go back.'

'Army guy?' Mark said after a pause.

'Yes, they were both in Afghanistan.'

Mark let her go and took a step back. He reached into his pocket for his cigarettes. She never could figure out how something inherently unhealthy could look sexy. He sucked the smoke in slowly and closed his eyes.

'That's not good,' he said, breathing out smoke.

'Do you know who it is?'

'You don't want to know.' He pulled her in for another kiss. Was this all fake? She pressed her head into his chest. This was getting messy.

'I'll have to let them know that he is on their case.'

'Can't your army man go to London?'

'They won't – not while they can still help people.'

'And the kids?'

'They've gone off the radar.'

The M25 curved ahead of them as the car sped through the Downs. There were a few lorries chugging away, otherwise the traffic was light. Norman put his foot down.

'Do you like danger?'

'What do you mean, Gov?' Steve was irritating. Everything he did or said came out of comic books, films, TV and games. *Gov*? That's what they said in police procedurals.

'I mean get the light out and stick it on the roof.'

At least he was efficient; he extracted the blue light from the glove compartment, opened the window and fixed it on top.

'Ready!' Norman could feel the young man bracing himself as he squeezed his foot down on the accelerator. 'The way I see it is that Iverson is too thick to be our man. But who told him to leave the keys in and how would they know what time and which van?'

'Logic dictates that someone in Birmingham saw the van leave and told them which van it was in.' Steve's voice sounded choppy and rigid.

'Does logic tell us how that information was imparted?'

'Yes, Gov.' Steve's head was unmoving, he was staring straight ahead.

Norman smiled, he was doing 120 mph, this was better than Brands Hatch. All the cars moved as they heard him coming up, just the odd dunce who didn't understand how to drive.

Steve moved his hand and pressed it up against the dashboard.

'You've never been this fast before?'

'Only on *Need for Speed*.'

'What?'

'*Need for Speed*'s a computer game.'

He eased his foot up a bit and slowed to just under 100 mph. The motor was purring now. No point giving Steve a heart attack, yet.

'You were talking about your logical deductions.'

'Yes, Gov, I deduce that we are looking for an email or more likely text alerting our man about what, when and where.'

'Yup.'

'I read this book once where the villain was apprehended when...'

'Steve, this is real life,' Norman cut in, 'if I take my hands off the wheel we don't reboot, we die.'

Norman let his hands float up above the steering wheel.

'Yes, Gov.' He was in the outside lane and there were no cars ahead, so he let them hover. 'Point made, Gov.'

'Steve, you have not lived much, have you?'

'I'm not sure what you mean.'

'You play a lot of computer games?'

'I am partial to them.'

'You like porn. Hard core.'

Steve looked out of the window. Norman waited, he could imagine it. Steve lived alone or maybe with his parents, his place was full of computer stuff, he was online all the time, he never went out and he sure as hell had never been with a woman.

'It's not illegal.' Steve said. 'What's your point, Gov?'

'Don't call me that. '

He overtook a Jaguar, that felt good.

'What, Gov?'

'Sir or boss will do.'

'Yes, boss.'

'My point is this: Steve you are very smart, but the real world doesn't operate on logic or along the lines of a nicely crafted game. The real world is ugly and you need to get down and dirty if you want to stay with the game.'

Maisie had a strange idea that just would not go away. It was those kids' books. Tom was up to something. He had kept Darcy out of the house, what did he have to hide and there was this family all over the news that had gone missing. It did not make sense but she had this gut feeling that it was no coincidence. That family had been at Ashford; Tom had gone to Ashford that day. He could have nabbed them up. He could have done it without Darcy knowing. She did not have to have been with him all the time. It seemed mad, but the more Maisie thought about it the stronger the certainty grew in her. She didn't want to get Darcy in trouble. They were mates. But she had a bad feeling about Tom, and if he had those kids… their mum was desperate. She knew what that felt like. When Jay had first done a runner with Jayde she thought she would die.

At lunchtime she texted her mum to remind her she was home that night. Her Twitter feed was all talk of kid-snatchers. There was a number to ring. Nah, it just wasn't likely, was it. She walked off towards the tunnels. She never walked nowhere during lunch break. When she was quite alone she copied and pasted the number and rang it.

'Home Security Hot Line.'

'Yeah, hi. About those missing kids.'

'The Dylans?'

'Yeah, them. It might not be much to go on but there is this bloke where I work, it's a strawberry farm, he's never had no kids but all of a sudden his curtains are drawn and there are kids' books in the living room. There ain't ever been a kid in there before, and the curtains ain't ever been closed before.'

'So, you have not actually seen them?'

'No, but I got this feeling. You know how sometimes, you just know.'

'I see.'

Maisie felt foolish.

'My friend, she…' Darcy had flown out of the shower in the morning and changed stations when the news bulletin was on.

'I'm sorry, I just thought it was a help.' She pressed the red button and disconnected. She was an idiot, never had much sense, what did she know?

She dialled her mother.

'Hi, it's me.'

'Hi, love.'

'How are the kids? Do they wanna talk?'

'Nah, they're fine. We're on the beach and they're mucking around. Tide's just turning. There's always stuff to find when it goes out.'

'Okay, I'll be back in time for a late dinner. Give 'em me love.'

She could not get the image of Darcy standing naked as the day she was born, the rivulets of water streaming down her, out of her head. Maybe she had changed the station deliberately, because of the news, she'd never wanted to dance before breakfast before. Nah, that couldn't be right. Tom was a shite, he could be mixed up in something, but not Darcy. If he was mixed up in this he could get her in trouble.

Norman had told Tess to have the chairs arranged theatre-style in rows. Not so the staff could see him, but so that he coul see them. It was a good thing he had brought Steve, there was stuff the super-nerd could do that he couldn't. Tess stood in front of the four rows of stacking chairs, they were already full. The rest of the security staff filing into the room had to stand around the sides. Norman watched their faces as they came in, he wanted to register any ,shock, twinge or blush. Steve was waiting in Tess's office. It was best if the staff were under the impression he was alone.

'Are we all here now?'

The heads all bounced up and down, nodding. There were a few growls of affirmation. Tess counted. She nodded at Norman.

'The reason we are all here is, as you have probably guessed, to assist BiG Home Security Agent Marshall. He is charged with investigating the abduction of the Dylan family.' She stepped away and indicated that he should take her place.

'The security of our nation, of our people, and of all our charges is paramount. Until we know who was behind this failure, the nation holds all of you responsible for this scandalous loss.'

All their faces were turned to him as he swept his gaze over them. They shifted in their seats, pulled themselves up. Tess slipped out of the back of the room as he had instructed.

'I have brought you all here, because together we are going to account for all of your movements on Tuesday morning. No one is leaving here until we have accounted for everyone's every move between 0500 and 1000 hours on Tuesday.' He let that sink in. 'Understood?' Nothing, no signs of obvious nervousness.

Norman was not worried. This part was a charade. Out of sight, Tess was opening all the staff lockers and Steve was unlocking all the mobile phones they found in them. They would look for anything, any phone call, any text, iMessage, Messenger, WhatsApp or Instagram message that came in before 10:28 on Tuesday with details of the van, or the family. Any clue. Steve's excitement had been unbearable. It was like a game, a challenge, and there was a time limit. Norman was certain that Steve could unlock the phones and hack into the accounts on them. He had not been daunted at all, just like a dog desperate to get off the leash.

'Could everyone take one of these time sheets and fill them in, minute by minute. We want to know where everyone was all the time and we are going to cross-reference all your movements. We want to know, who you saw, when and where. If you fill in the form correctly we can let you get back to work.'

He smiled. He could tie them up for hours by cross-referencing them one by one in public. He could rely on inconsistencies and errors to keep them here long enough for Steve and Tess to check all the phones. The only person being tortured today would be him – by tedium. Tess could make up for that later.

The doorbell rang. No one rang Cordelia's door at this time of day. Everyone was in the fields. Cordelia pushed back her chair. With luck it would be someone to collect the family.

Tom was standing on the doorstep.

'Good morning, Mrs Hughes.'

'Oh, come in, Tom. Do come in.'

She looked over his shoulder. That fat girl – Mary? Marcy? Macy? – was scuttling away towards the poly-tunnels. Had she been watching?

'Did you hear the news?' Tomasz said as soon as the door was closed.

'Of course.'

'And your contact, the priest?'

The priest? Priest. He meant Vicars. Tomasz was talking in code now.

'Oh, you mean?'

Tom lifted his fingers to his pursed lips.

'No, I missed my appointment with him. I heard that he was talking to someone else about church security. Why don't you join me on the patio for a drink?'

There was no reason to suppose that they were being bugged, but anything was possible in this day and age. The house was on the top of the Greensand ridge which fell away onto the Weald. From the patio you could see the lush fields and woodland of the Weald, a gentle valley stretching away as far as the High Weald and in the distance behind were the South Downs. On a windy day the prevailing winds rushed up the over the neat lines of white poly-tunnels in the strawberry fields and emerged in a blast over the patio. The patio was an architectural disaster but made a perfect haven for secretive conversations.

Cordelia had maintained the family tradition of making apple and pear juice from the windfall crop every autumn. She extracted an open bottle of pear juice from the fridge, while Tom fetched glasses from the cabinet. They worked well together as a team, in everything. She watched him as she poured the juice out before she sat down.

'You look different.'

'How?'

'Despite the worry, you look happy.'

'Things are good, personally.'

'Darcy?'

He hesitated before replying. 'Is it that obvious?'

'Only to me. I know you both well.'

'You don't mind? We won't let it interfere.'

'God no, I think it's fantastic. You should have got together ages ago.'

'I agree.' He sipped some juice then fixed his eyes on her. 'I met Alfie.'

Cordelia raised her eyebrows.

'He's great. She's done well,' he said.

'She has, especially considering.'

'These... circumstances.'

'Yes, which brings us to our errant priest. I was told yesterday that he was "having talks".'

'By who?'

'Someone I barely know. She said it in such a way that I could only think she meant being interrogated.'

'That would explain a lot. Have you tried ringing him?'

'I've rung all his numbers, sent him emails, Whatsapped, you name it. All I could say was sorry to miss you at the reception yesterday.'

'What about the contact, the woman who told you he was having talks?'

'Sandy Melsom? I thought she was just a socialite. I'm not sure.'

'We've got to move them though, they can't stay here. Maisie's been snooping around.'

'She was watching when you came in here.'

Norman had asked for the room he used for getting people to talk. The guards all knew what went on in there. The bucket was full of water. It was tepid; they must have filled it first thing. The two piles of newspaper were still under the table from last time. All he had to do was lift the table legs at one end onto them and he was ready to go. It was not a professional set up but all he needed was an inclined surface to hold the interviewee down on, straps and water. Cling film and a cloth to put over the face were handy but not essential. They could save a lot of time, as well as prevent him from getting wet. The feeble usually started blubbering and spilling the beans when their mouths were cling filmed. That set off enough panic in most. The tough ones, even they could not help struggling as their airways filled up with water. That's when he got soaked, when they struggled even though they were tied down. He was hoping that whoever Tess brought in through that door would not be a splasher.

Steve had unlocked all the phones they had found. There was nothing. Then the boy wonder had gone and checked all the toilets. He had obviously seen lots of movies where phones were hidden behind, in or on top of toilet cisterns. The trouble with Ashford was that it had been a modern purpose-built shopping mall, the cisterns were all buried in the wall. But, Steve had still looked around and found the phone inside an unfilled soap dispenser. It was a brick phone; single purpose, no stored numbers. There were just two messages on it.

The first message was: *BM20MRS*. It was a vehicle registration number. It still pissed him off that the Londoners had reverted to the traditional registration style after BiG had kept DVLA to itself. He liked tradition and had never warmed to the new registration system. Someone had said that Charlie boy had come up with the idea. What was it? A royal decree?

And the second message *10:15–30*. He did not need to be Einstein to understand that was the registration number of the transport that brought the Dhillons down from Birmingham and the second message was the ETA. Fuck. They had someone working in Re-Migration Service's Transit Department – but not Iverson; he was too thick to even cover his own tracks. Someone in Birmingham who knew what time they left, their ETA, what van they were in and could get a message to someone in Ashford. The trouble was there were no fingerprints on the phone. Steve had checked it over. Whoever had used the phone was smart, he or she had not taken it off the camp, nor binned it, nor used anything that could trace it back to him or herself. Again, it could not be Iverson.

It was a pain but they could not pin the phone on anyone. The door opened and Tess walked in with a guard. It was a man, mid-30s, slight paunch, short hair to mask his receding hair line.

'This is Neil Seddon. I'll be in my office if you need me.'

Seddon did not look especially apprehensive; nervous yes, but not terrified.

'Seddon, is it?' Norman pulled out a chair from the table. He sat down. There was no chair for Seddon.

'Yes. Neil Seddon.'

'So, Mr Seddon, your story does not add up. I'm interested in ten minutes between 10:21 and 10:32 to be precise. Your log shows that you were with Dave Green until 10:22 and then went to the bathroom and then got a coffee from the main office at 10:25 and then went to relieve the guards at the barrier at 10:30.'

'Yes, that's right – more or less.'

'More or less?'

'Well I wasn't timing my movements. It's what I do every day.'

Norman stared at Seddon and said nothing. The man shifted his weight from one foot to the other.

'The trouble, Mr Seddon,' Norman spoke with deliberate softness, 'is that no one can verify that you got that cup of coffee. There were five people in the office, three drinking coffee and not one of them recalls seeing you.'

'But I did.'

'No one can corroborate your movements between 10:22 and 10:30.'

'I'm not lying.'

Norman got up and walked to the end of the table.

'Are you sure?' He lifted the table legs onto the piles of newspaper. They were high enough to give just the right tilt to the table, enough to stop the interrogee from being drowned.

Now there was a look of panic in Seddon's eyes.

'That's what I did. I took a slash, grabbed a coffee and went over to the gatehouse.'

'So why did no one see you?'

Norman picked up the bucket and moved it to the head of the table, careful not to spill any water.

Seddon seemed to shrink. Fight or flight. This was the moment you could tell a man. The adrenalin would be pumping round him now. Was he going to get aggressive or panic. He was looking more red than white.

'It's just like I said.'

Tiny beads of sweat were running down his forehead. His hands had retracted into fists. Interesting. Norman had had him down for flight.

'You know what's going to happen next?'

Maisie hated the journey home. It was a slog. If she'd had a car she could have done it in an hour. But she had no money to spare, even the bus fares were a stretch. She hitched a lift with one of the chiller lorries stuffed with the supermarket-ready crates of strawberries. The driver dropped her at her first bus stop. She knew the route from staring out of the window all the way. She never slept on the bus, however tired she was, she was too frightened of missing her stops. They trundled past

Snodland Working Men's Club, the white paint looked dirty, the windows all closed. It was a way to go before she had to change bus; at least another hour and a half before she got home. It felt like for ever.

She ought to be feeling happy. She ought to be excited at the prospect of seeing the kids and eating some decent grub, but she was not. She was right to have made that call; but why then did she feel like some low life scum? What really got her goat was that her brain was like some random YouTube selection; she kept on seeing flashes of Darcy's body, her breasts when she was pulling her top on, her backside all shiny and wet when she came out the shower. Bloody hell was she turning into some kind of lesbo? Maybe she just wasn't getting enough? It happened to women in prison. It's not like there weren't any men around, after all there was Tom and there were plenty of other blokes picking. It was just since Jay. Since he had gone to St Lucia, she just had not had the heart. Anyway, she had to work. She had Tyler and Molly to look after, as well as her mum. She couldn't risk getting knocked up again. And nothing would ever make up for losing Jayde. It was better just to keep her legs crossed. Still didn't explain it; she just couldn't get Darcy out of her mind.

No one was in when she got back home. Maisie walked through the house, there was no sign of nobody. The cushions on the settee in the front room were all puffed up and pristine like her mum liked it. The TV was off. The kitchen was clean and tidy. There was no sign of supper. She looked through the window. The washing on the line was just clothes. No swimming stuff. They were always back from the beach before five. She opened the fridge. There were two pizzas from the Co-op, a lettuce, cherry tomatoes and carrots. They hadn't eaten tea.

She walked down the road as far as the bus stop. It was stupid. There was no point her going off. Most likely they had just gone down to Minnis Bay and walked along from the sailing club; Tyler loved the boats. If it was windy Mum sometimes went down to Epple Bay, it was more sheltered and the kids liked playing on the rocky platform as they walked back under the cliff. She rang her mum's mobile again.

She had taken all the clothes off the line, folded and ironed them and put them away when she heard a car drive up outside. She was at the door before the car engine had turned off. It was a police car. Jeez. She raced out. The driver door opened. A woman PC got out.

'Evening. You Miss Wilson?'

'Yeah, that's me. What's happened?'

'Ah, nothing much. But your mum can't get out. Molly's asleep on her lap.' The policewoman opened the door behind her and Tyler jumped out.

'Mummy, Mummy. I've been in a police car and the police-woman put the siren on. It was so loud.'

She scooped him up in her arms and held him tight.

The policewoman was at the other side of the car, she was levering her mum up and out. Mum was clutching Molly in her arms. Molly's face was all pink and soft and asleep. She knew that look. They were safe.

Darcy stood next to her mum looking out the kitchen window rubbing the flour, butter and sugar together in a bowl, while her mum cut up the strawberries for the crumble. They didn't talk much but both were watching Alfie and Tom kick a ball around in the garden. While they listened to the radio. Her mother never seemed to turn it off.

'*Mrs Albury from Shelford do you agree with the last caller that hanging is medieval and barbaric?*' the host said in her smooth, plummy voice.

'*Hello, Isabelle, no, well yes, I have a problem with the spectacle. I don't see why these people should not be dispatched like the animals that they are away from the lights and publicity.*'

'*You mean with stun guns in a slaughter house?*'

'*No, no. We could electrocute them, or inject them, something quick and painless but none of this public stuff. Hanging is no better than beheading or shooting and we are not like them, you know.*'

'Them!' Darcy turned the radio off. 'Who is them? Anyone who is Verified Not British. Oh, Mum.'

Her mum put down the knife and the strawberries. She put her arm round Darcy's shoulder. They watched Alfie and Tom playing in the soft late afternoon light.

'He's good with him,' her mum said.

'He's a good man.'

'Reckon he is. Worth the wait it seems.'

As she walked down the lawn, towards the bottom of the slope where they were playing, a strange, unfamiliar feeling seemed to spread over her whole being. She was happy. It was a long time since she had felt so much at peace and yet so excited. She bent to kiss Alfie but he ran away.

'Mummy, I'm playing.' That was a first.

Tomasz smiled at her.

'Supper's ready,' she said.

They walked up the hill. Hand in hand while Alfie ran ahead.

This time Tom stayed downstairs with her mum and helped clear up while she put Alfie to bed. When she got down they were sitting in the front room, tennis on the television and mugs of tea with chalky shiny scum floating on the top.

'Hi, love. I was just telling Tom about how Cordelia and I go back.'

'Yeah, it's amazing to think you've known her since you were kids,' Tomasz said.

'Yeah, Granddad was in charge of the pickers for Cordelia's dad.'

'I'm a few years older but my mum worked in her house and Cordelia and I, well we used to play together.' Her mum reached for her tea, looked at it before putting it back down. 'I guess I kept her out of everyone's hair. Later, when my mum died, I started cleaning for Mrs Hughes and then later for Cordelia.'

'So, you're like family?'

'Oh no. Not family, nor friends. But something else, we're just close.' Her mum got up and grabbed the mugs. 'These are all cold. I'll make some more.'

'What's that about?' Tom asked after she was gone.

'Later.' Darcy raised her fingers to her lips. 'I'll tell you later,' she whispered before continuing loudly, 'Mum had to stop when Alfie came along. It made more sense for me to work, and Mum to stay home. That's when Cordelia gave us this place.'

'She's been good to us,' her mum shouted from the kitchen.

Tess's flat was pristine, as usual. Norman put the pizza boxes on the kitchen counter and wondered if Tess ever had any other visitors. It must be hard in her line of work to meet people she could socialise with; not her staff, not her 'clients'. All the better for him; he could pop round whenever he wanted to. The kitchen surfaces were white and shiny, there was nothing left out, just a single rose in a clear thin vase by the window. Flowers were much more expensive these days, they were mainly imported from Holland. Who would have thought the price of romance would have gone up because of independence? The rose was dying, one crimson petal lay on the work top.

'Come in,' Tess said to Steve who had not moved beyond the doormat.

'I thought you would not mind a working dinner,' Norman said.

'Not at all, does that mean no wine?' Tess pulled out a wine bottle from a rack under the work top.

'Can't have pizza without wine, can we?' Norman took the cork screw from her and speared the cork with it.

Tessa placed three large glasses in a row.

'Steve,' Norman gestured at the knife block, 'you sort out the pizza.'

Steve half-pulled the knives out one by one until he found the serrated one; he drew it out. Norman took a big gulp of wine, enjoying the warm sensation as it slid down.

'So, what did you get from Neil Seddon?' Tess's ice-blue eyes met his gaze.

Norman put the wine glass down. She had balls, he liked that.

'Nothing, precisely nothing. If you ask me his story holds up because he is such a nobody; no one noticed where he was. He's just boring. Did you know he worked in a few of the shops here before?'

'Yes. I didn't have him down for a terrorist,' Tess looked down at the table, 'he's a good member of staff.'

'He doesn't fit the profile,' Steve said.

'Can't be helped. I can't afford to miss anything. He'll recover.'

'Look on the bright side, he'll have something to talk about next week,' Steve said.

'It's not a joke.' If looks could kill, Tess had shot Steve dead.

'I didn't mean it like that. Honestly.' Steve blushed, Tess stared him down.

'Hey, we're on the same side here,' Norman said. 'It was unfortunate, he's collateral. We know it has to be someone else on the staff.'

'Well I still have to go through all the camp videos. I could start here.' Steve turned to Tess. 'Have you got WiFi?'

Norman closed the bedroom door. It was strangely exciting, knowing that Steve was out there working, possibly listening, and he had this beautiful, compliant woman just with a thin partition wall between them.

'Come here.'

He grabbed her and kissed her hard.

'Don't move. You're going to do everything I command. To the letter.'

Jenny had made him watch the DVD of *50 Shades* years ago. He knew what to do.

'Empty out that bedside drawer onto the bed. Neatly.'

He waited until she had laid out the contents of her secret trove on the grey satin bed cover.

'Put on the blindfold', he said.

He stripped her piece by piece. He pulled, unfastened and then dropped or draped her shirt, skirt, slip, bra, tights and thong over her white gilt chair. She tensed each time he touched her.

He studied the kinky gear on the bed. He put the handcuffs and the paddle back in the drawer, they were too much like work. He picked up the nipple clamps.

She cried out as he fastened them.

'I said be quiet.' It was a stupid fiddly business. 'Get on the bed.'

He tied her wrists and ankles with the four satin restraints to the headboard and the legs at the end of the bed. He was left with some thick pink tape, a black silk cord, an anal plug, a black leather flogger – which reminded him of the over-sized tassels on the black velvet tie-backs Jenny had bought for the living room curtains – and a large pink feather. He picked up the feather. He brushed it down between her small breasts, she shuddered. He flicked it again, she gasped. Sex with Jenny was much less complicated. He picked up the anal plug, she trembled and groaned as he shoved it in. He broke off a few inches of tape and sealed her mouth. Then he played with the flogger. It was hard to tell if she liked it, it left a red mark each time he slapped it against her but her writhing did not continue. She was not struggling to break loose like Neil Seddon had. He couldn't even suck her breasts because the clamps were in the way. Maybe he should simply get down and shaft her?

There was a double knock on the door.

'What?'

'Sorry Gov, but it's urgent.' Steve's voice was muffled by the door.

'You wait here,' he told Tess, 'not a squeak. I'll be back in a jiffy.'

Steve was standing in front of the door, his hand poised to knock again. The look on Steve's face as he caught sight of Tess on the bed gave Norman more pleasure than anything he had done in the last twenty minutes.

Maisie left the kids' bedroom door slightly ajar and listened. She waited. Nothing. They were out cold, they'd had too much excitement. She had taken Molly up straight away. She had held her on the toilet and flopped her down straight into bed, wriggled her clothes off her without Molly even waking. Tyler had been beside himself; he'd cried because his pizza slice was too big or too small; he'd cried when she said he had to go to bed; he'd cried brushing his teeth; he'd cried climbing the ladder to his bunk, and had been asleep within a minute of putting his head on his pillow, still crying.

Her mum was sat at the kitchen table. The cup of tea she had made for herself after supper was untouched.

'What happened?' Maisie sat down opposite her mum.

Her mum looked at her. She hadn't seen her this upset since Jayde had gone.

'What, Mum?'

Her mum seemed to fold in on herself, her arms and shoulders all caved forwards and then she started shaking. She was sobbing. She reached across the table.

'It's all right, we're all here, Mum, we're all safe.'

'No, we're not. None of us is fuckin' safe no more. None of us.' She rubbed her red eyes. 'It's wrong, so bleeding wrong.'

'What, Mum? Tell me.'

'We were on the beach this afternoon, down beyond the huts, the tide had just turned, when Tyler came running back, saying he'd found a dead man. By the time I had got to where he was pointing there were two. A man and a girl. I rang the police. They came. They took us back to Margate Police Station.'

'That makes sense.'

'The police were fine. They asked us what we'd seen and then they made me sign this form.'

'What form?'

'The new Official Secrets form. I ain't meant to be telling you any of this. I ain't meant to have seen what I saw.'

'Tell me what? That you saw two drowned people?'

'We're breaking the law. Right now.'

'That's mental, Mum.'

'The thing is the man and the girl... they weren't white.'

'What do you mean?'

'They were black. Like Jay. And Jayde.'

'I don't understand.'

'What really got me was the van that came to collect the bodies wasn't the police, nor the funeral parlour, it was Re-Migration services.'

'This better be good,' Norman waited for Steve to look away before he closed the door behind him. Steve's face was red.

'It's the duty manager from the Home Security Hot Line. She won't speak to me. She insisted on speaking to you. Her name is Helen Smith.'

Steve held out Norman's mobile. Norman had left it next to the bottle of wine. He hadn't wanted Jenny interrupting him.

'Agent Norman Marshall speaking.'

'Sorry to interrupt you this late, sir, but I think we had a call earlier today that might be helpful in the Dhillon case. I am sorry it's significance may have been missed earlier.'

Norman put the phone on speaker. As soon as the duty manager mentioned the strawberry farm Steve opened his laptop. He tapped and slid his finger over the mouse pad with alacrity and spun the laptop round to display the photo of a van passing through the barrier at Ashford Transit Camp. C H Fruits and the image of a strawberry was on the side of the van.

'What did you say the name of the farm was?'

'We didn't get the name but we've got the GPS coordinates.'

Steve typed them in as quickly as the manager spoke.

'Bingo,' Steve said, 'that can't be a coincidence. C H Fruit Farms.'

'It was Helen Smith, wasn't it? I'm going get to you a commendation for your work. Stellar stuff. Email me everything you have as soon as we're done talking.'

Norman filled the kettle. It was going to be a long night and he needed to be alert. He had a lot of calls to make. Damn Tess, it was impossible to find anything in her kitchen, even the coffee was hidden behind a white door. He sighed. She was still on her bed. He put two spoons of instant coffee in his mug and two of sugar. The granules disappeared as he poured the water in, the water darkened instantaneously. Steve was hunched over his laptop.

He would wager that Steve did porn because he was a virgin. He didn't have the confidence or where-with-all to chat a woman up, an avatar in some game maybe, but not in the flesh. Steve needed a fuck. Norman needed to work. This S&M thing really did not work for him.

'Steve, I'll just be a minute.'

In the bedroom Tess was as he had left her. She could not be any other way. He sat down on the bed and uncovered her eyes.

'There've been developments. There's some good news. We think we've found the Dhillon family. I've got to work. But I've an idea. I don't think Steve has ever done it. Had sex. Do you think you could make a man of him?'

Her blue eyes stared at him. He waited. Then slowly she nodded. Once, then again.

'Shall I untie you?'

She nodded.

He peeled the tape off her lips. They looked flushed and tender.

'Leave the rest. Send him in to do the rest. But kiss me first.'

Norman felt quite pleased with himself as he returned to the kitchen. This would change Steve's life. He would be less of a prick to deal with. Steve looked up from his laptop.

'There's something I need you to do for me.' He took a sip of coffee, it was scalding.

'Anything, Gov.'

'I preferred boss.'

'Yes, sorry. Anything, boss.'

'You've done a good day's work. You've proved your worth. I like to reward people for their contributions. I've been thinking about our conversation in the car, on the way down. It's a bit awkward, but you know I need to make some calls and get on the case.'

'Yes.'

'Well, I can't really leave Tess like that. I think you know what I mean.'

Steve's face turned red.

'You would do me a favour if you could go in and help her. She'll tell you what to do.'

'Help her? In there?'

Norman walked over to the door to Tess's bedroom. He opened it and beckoned Steve over. Steve walked over like a robot.

'Come in,' Tess said.

Norman put his hand on Steve's shoulder to propel him into the room, the heat coming off him told him he was very much alive. Norman meant what he said; this was the reward Steve needed.

He shut the door.

Later, much later, when their bodies were entwined and Darcy had lost any sense of which limb was whose or where hers were, when she was drifting in and out of sleep, struggling not to close her eyes, Tomasz opened his.

'You were going to tell me what upset your mum before.'

'Oh, it's about Alfie and his dad.'

Tomasz's eyes were steady. Hazel green and bright. 'You can tell me. I want to know everything about you.'

Darcy levered herself back a little, to see Tom better. 'Did you know that Cordelia had a brother?'

'He lives abroad or something?'

'Yeah, when old Mr Hughes died she bought her brother, Ray, out of the business and he went to Brazil and started up his own strawberry farm there.'

'Can't get away from strawberries.'

She had to kiss him; she could not get away from his lips. 'Where was I?'

'Ray's Brazilian strawberry farm.' Darcy wondered if Tomasz smelt of strawberries. She nuzzled him but he pushed her back.

'Okay. One Christmas, I was fifteen, Ray turns up with his Brazilian wife and her son, by her first marriage. He was two years older than me, so Cordelia asked me to show him around. Luiz was like his mum, just as beautiful but darker. We hung out a lot and one thing led to another.'

'Were you in love with him?'

'Love? Dunno. I thought so at the time. It was romantic. He had never been cold, never seen snow (we had a freak snow storm), he was just excited. It was charming. He spoke with this lovely, lilting accent, his pronunciation was shite. You know Brazilians can't finish words on hard sounds.'

'What?'

'Oh, like field, they say fieldgie, or hat becomes hattie; it's funny.'

She smiled, remembering. Tomasz's body was rigid like a block of wood in her arms.

'The thing is, Tomasz, I barely knew him. It was romantic an' all but that's all it was: a romance, a fairy tale. But this,' she gave him a shower of tiny kisses over his face, 'this is different. I've watched you, I know you, I get you.'

They could not sleep. They were lying dazed but awake.

'What happened to Luiz?'

'He went home after six weeks. It was their summer holiday.'

'And you?'

'I thought my heart would break. And then my period didn't come and that's when the shit hit the fan. My mum was beside herself, my dad tried to talk me into an abortion one day and the next he wanted to get money from Ray, Cordelia's brother. I decided I wasn't going to have an abortion.'

Tom was silent, his lips touched her forehead like a reflex. 'Alfie's four?'

'Yeah,' she kissed him back properly.

'You were pregnant,' he pulled away, 'when they started talking about the Britishness laws?'

'Exactly.'

'Weren't you frightened?'

'Of course, I was. When Luiz found out that I was pregnant there was all this talk of getting married and going to live in Brazil. That's when I realised that it was just a dream, a romance like I said. I didn't want to go. I wanted to keep the baby. Then Cordelia came up with this plan. We live here, rent free, my mum looks after Alfie and schools him, and I work on the farm. Like my mum says, not friends, not family but all messed up together. Except, I like Cordelia for real.'

'But Alfie can't stay here, alone, for ever.'

'I know. We've got to get out.'

'Brazil?'

'No. The last few days I've been thinking of somewhere closer.' She kissed him again, 'How does Poland sound to you?'

She liked the way his face broke into a smile without a moment's hesitation.

Minus Three: Friday

It took for ever for Maisie to get to sleep. She kept on thinking about the bodies on the beach. A man and a girl. A father and a daughter maybe. Black. Like Jay and Jayde. She knew it wasn't them. He had run off to St Lucia years ago. 'I'm just taking her for two weeks, spend Christmas with my family'. Right. She was dumb to fall for that one. Two weeks that became for ever. But maybe, if he had not scarpered with her, it could have been them. It was like them at least.

She got out of bed at least three times, telling herself she would sleep better if she had a pee; but each time she ended up peering into the kids' room, waiting until her eyes had got used to the dark and she could see Tyler and Molly, see their covers going up and down like boats on the sea. Poor little girl. Poor dad.

She didn't know how long she had been asleep when she heard her phone buzzing. It was charging on the bedside table but she always put it in vibrate mode before she slept. Now it was bloody well dancing along. *Buzz. Buzz.* She ignored it. No one would ring her at this hour. Got to be a missed call. After a few buzzes more it stopped. Thank you! *Buzz. Buzz.* It started again. She counted to eight. It stopped and she rolled onto her back, awake again. *Buzz.* She grabbed the phone and swiped across the screen.

'Who the fuck do you think you are, ringing me at this time?'

'So sorry. This is Agent Norman Marshall of Home Security. And I am speaking to whom?'

'What?'

'Did you ring the Home Security Hot Line yesterday?'

'Yesterday? Yes.'

'And what's your name?'

'Maisie Wilson.'

'I apologise, Miss Wilson, for ringing this early'

'What time is it?'

'01:56 a.m.'

'Two o'clock! This better be good.'

'Well, I think it was your call that was good. We need to follow up on some details. When you rang and spoke to our agent you didn't say which house you saw the books in. Or which strawberry farm.'

'Oh, in… they were in...' She could see the children's books scattered on the floor of Tom's living room, she remembered crying like a baby afterwards, and then there was her mum crying about the little girl on the beach. 'I am sure it was nothing. It was just some kid's books.'

'Yes, we understand it might seem like nothing and it was just a hunch, but I have a hunch that you might be right.'

'Oh. I can't think. Can we talk in the morning?'

'No, Miss Wilson, it is rather urgent that you tell me which house it is.'

'Can't it wait?'

'Well, you could go back to sleep or I could double the number of Home Security and Re-Migration Service Agents I have heading toward C H Fruit Farms and they could search every property, wake everyone up and, of course, I could mention to them all who made the phone call. Or you can tell me which house the children's books were in and you will never hear from us again. Unless you want a BiG Good Citizenship Commendation in the Best of Britain Annual Awards?'

It was Ro's third night hiding in Tom's house but the first night that he had a bed to sleep in. Tom was staying the night at Darcy's and said if Ro didn't mind his sheets not being clean he could kip in his bed. There was only so many *movies4men* and sport he could watch. But he could not sleep. It wasn't the smell of Tom on the sheets, it wasn't because it was too hot, he just could not stop worrying. From what they had told him there was this guy they called the Priest who arranged everything. But the Priest was laying low, had gone into hiding or something and it was the Priest who told them where to go for transfers and stuff. So much for The Terrorists or The Resistance. As far as he could make out it was a hobby for some kindly folks in their spare time and they were not very good at it. Not that he could complain. He would be stuck in Ashford or on some train now if they had not gotten him out. But the kids didn't get it, they were getting really bored and testy. And he did not feel safe. He didn't want the children to realise anything was wrong, but the way Kiran was hushing the other two... he knew something was up. He was a smart boy. God, he was proud of him. And Kirsty, how could she? After they had seen her on telly he had to hide the phone to stop them ringing her.

He must have slept a bit because the next time he looked at the clock, the numbers 03:48 were flashing. The small hours always passed slowly: 03:49. He rolled onto his back. Fear rose up through his gut, he felt sick. He sat up. He could not let this fear dominate him. He fell on the floor and did fifty push-ups. He wasn't going to go back to sleep, he might as well read. Tom had blackout curtains; he could not tell if it was still dark outside. He pulled the blue material back. Dawn. He could barely see the garden, just the shapes and tones; it was colourless. Maybe he should go for a run. There would be nobody out now, no one to ask questions and the kids would sleep through for another couple of hours. He opened the window to gauge the temperature.

It was still warm and sultry but the air was fresh compared to Brummie air. He inhaled deep into his chest; no fumes. He held his breath. There were voices on the breeze; hushed whispers, short staccato orders. He pulled the curtain over his face, leaving enough gap to see out. How had he not seen them? There were ninja-types swarming around the garden making a circle. He stepped back tugging the drape back to the middle.

The kids were still asleep and did not even stir when he rushed past to peer through their curtains at the front. The same, a cordon of police or Home Security or fuck knows who – but they were surrounded. Think. Think. Tom had an attic. He could get them all up there and hide out. There was no way they could get out.

'Kiran.' He shook his shoulder. 'Kiran, wake up.'

'What?' The boy's voice was thick with sleep.

'They're here. We've got to hide.'

Kiran sat up. 'Who?'

'I dunno. The police. They're all around the house. We got to hide.'

'There's nowhere.'

'The attic. You got to help me get the little ones up there and keep them quiet.'

Kiran looked as if he was about to cry, but then he jumped onto his brother and sister.

'Maya. Neel. Dad wants us to play silent hide and seek. Come quick.'

Maya and Neel could barely move, it was like they were drugged but Kiran got them out of bed while Ro worked out how to get the loft ladder down. Strangely their sleepiness helped, they followed instructions like robots. Ro threw up the duvet and their bags which they had not even unpacked and then scrambled up after them.

The ladder was designed to retract from below and it was fiddly pulling it up behind them. The trap door had nothing to grab hold of from above. Ro pitched forward but could not reach as far as the front.

'Kiran, sit on my legs.'

As soon as he felt Kiran's weight on his outstretched legs he extended himself as far as he could and reached his fingertips down the sides of the trapdoor. He just had to lever himself and the trap door up.

He walked his fingers down the sides as he pulled the door up. The edges dug into his fingers, he could just about hold it up, but he could not close it. His fingers were in the way of him closing it. He was breathing heavily. He could sense the children were not asleep, that they were watching.

The weird dawn quiet was shattered by the crash and creak of wood shattering and glass breaking downstairs. The front and back doors, he guessed. If he could just get that trap door up.

The house was full of noise, of the sound of voices and feet thumping around below them. 'Ground floor clear. Upstairs. Now,' someone shouted.

The thud of feet on the stairs started up immediately. He pressed hard, keeping the door up. He pulled the door higher, his fingers jammed against the wooden rim of the trap, he couldn't move them and lost his grip. For a second the door seemed to defy gravity and then it flapped back open. A masked face looked right up at him and then there were torches blinding him.

'Daddy,' Neel's voice came from behind him, 'the men aren't playing nicely. They sound very angry.'

Maisie sat at her mother's kitchen table and watched the dawn break. Her mug of tea stopped steaming. She was used to waking up early for picking. They were in the fields by five. But she usually slept like a log until her alarm went off. It had still been dark when she came downstairs. She had sat in the dark. Now she could see everything, but it was like all the colour had been drained out of the world. The kitchen looked like it had been painted in blue. There was no red. It was lifeless. Like the bodies on the beach. She got up and chucked the cold tea down the sink. She refilled the kettle, leaning against the worktop, looking out into the garden while the kettle hummed and then rumbled. She made tea. Then she was stirring in a sugar but she couldn't remember if she had put any in already.

She checked the news feeds from the local newspaper. There was nothing about the bodies. Her mum had heard rumours, that other people had seen bodies, but she hadn't believed them. We don't do stuff like that. This is England. That's what she had thought, that's why she had rung the Hot Line yesterday. But now?

That guy, Agent Marshall, he had been polite but threatening. He had right scared her. Decent and nasty all rolled into one. Fuck. What had she done? The tea would go cold if she didn't drink it. With the price of teabags these days, she shouldn't waste it. She took a sip.

She swiped her phone again. Nothing on the NBBC Kent newsfeed. Nothing on Heart Radio. Nothing ever happened here, normally if you so much as stepped out of the pub drunk in Birchington, it was in the local news next day. The only way no one was talking about it was because the coppers didn't want people to know. And the police were just the messenger. This had to come down from on top. To be honest she never paid much attention to politics and all that. Never thought it mattered, but the idea of her kids seeing a little girl dead on the beach...

She slid her finger down through her contacts. She flicked up and then back down. Some names had photos of smiling faces attached. There was Jay. She tapped his new profile picture, enlarging it. His face was thinner, his skin darker – must be all that sun there; but his cheeky grin – that was the same. He tried ringing her sometimes. There was no wi-fi on his granddad's farm where he was, he could only ring if he was visiting family in town. He never had much to say but Jayde would tell her about her new friends, the school, the beach. He would have known what to do now.

She missed him. A tear ran down her face; she was going soft now. She hated it when he used to say that he was the love of her life. 'Why can't you say it the other way around. Like I'm the love of your life?' 'Because' he would reply and then kiss her. He knew it wound her up something rotten. And now he was gone. And Jayde. But what was worst, was that he was right. They were safe. Jayde was safe. She'd had Tyler and Molly after, but it still didn't stop her missing Jayde and her dad. And Tyler and Molly's dads? Jay was right, he was the one.

She swiped up and then down, the names scrolling by so fast like a fruit machine she didn't know where it would settle. She scrolled more slowly and then let her finger hover. There was no picture, just a name: Darcy. She pressed the green call button. The phone rang. It rang and then went to message. She pressed the red button, then the green call button again. This time Darcy picked up.

'Maisie? What's up?'

'Listen, I've got to tell you something and it is really important.'

'Couldn't it wait? It's not even four yet!'

'No. I think Tom might have been nabbed in a raid.'

'What do you mean?'

'I think the police have raided his house. They think those kids are there; you know, the Dhillon family.'

'What? How do you know?'

'I... I was worried about you. I just wanted to make sure you weren't there.'

'I better go. Thanks.' Darcy hung up.

Maisie listened to the flat tone then pressed the red button. She put the phone face down. She did not move from the table until she got up to throw the cold tea away. It was another beautiful bright summer's day. The kids would want to go to the beach.

Cordelia was dreaming that her door bell was ringing.

Ring. Riiiiinnnnggg. Thud. Thud.

She opened her eyes. She was not dreaming; the bell was ringing. Persistently. And someone was banging on the door. She sat up. Dawn was breaking. She had slept with her curtains open ever since Alan had died. She felt less cut off. This was the sort of thing when she missed him; middle of the night emergencies had been his department. Her alarm clock showed 3:57. Most of the staff would be getting up by now, some showering early to avoid the rush after 4 a.m. She wrapped her dressing gown round her as she went downstairs.

'Coming!'

What could be so urgent? It was probably the boiler or something else in the camp. She opened the door and shut her mouth. There were two Home Security Agents in black, with riot masks pushed back over their heads and a plain clothes agent in front of her.

'Mrs Hughes?'

'Yes, what's going on?'

Behind them at the end of the drive there were more agents, floodlit in the beam of their vans, which were parked up against her delivery trucks. The doors of one of the trucks were fanned open, an agent in a white forensic suit stepped out of it.

'Well that's what we would like to ask you, Mrs Hughes. I'm Home Security Agent Norman Marshall. I'm in charge of this investigation.'

Suddenly something Keith had told her came to mind. 'If they ever find you, don't act as if you know nothing, make yourself know nothing, forget everything. Be what you would have been if you hadn't got involved.' Right, she had better forget everything.

She took a step outside.

'What on earth is going on? That's one of my vans you've got people looking at. Who gave you the key and what's this all about?'

'Can we come in and talk, Mrs Hughes?'

'No. I'm not decent. You can wait in the lounge if you want or here. But I'm getting dressed.'

The man called Marshall looked a bit surprised. He was a big man, about fifty, grey hair closely cropped, looked like he kept fit. A man's man. Feminine wiles would do better than standing up to him.

'If that is all right with you, Agent Marshall?'

'We can wait. We're not going anywhere.' He turned away from her and shouted, 'Steve!'

A man peeled himself off from the crowd by the van and walked over carrying his laptop held against his chest. Cordelia turned and closed the door.

They would be tapping her phones by now or monitoring any mobile signals. If they were here she had to assume the worst: that, somehow, someone had tipped them off. The family must be gone. Oh, those poor kids. And Tomasz. Oh God, he and Darcy had just found each other. Know nothing.

She checked over her desk. She had been doing her accounts last night. She would never forgive herself if her real accounts were found. Of course, she had put her father's old ledger book away, as she always did. But for good measure she put it at the bottom of the drawer under a stash of old papers and letters. She grabbed her father's fountain pen. She would not want them to match the ink.

Darcy was at the farm at 4:30 like any normal day. Jane and Amy were getting dressed. They did not ask where she had been. People were like that here. The only way to get any privacy, living like this on top of one another, was to make it. People were deliberately blind, didn't ask questions, didn't pry. That's not the same as not saying nothing, there was plenty of gossip. She glanced at their bunk, only one bed had been slept in. She was not surprised. Probably the first time that they had had the room to themselves. They would not complain about her not being there.

She got changed and then made her way to the office. Even though she had an idea she still came to a stand when she turned the corner into the courtyard in front of the office. Usually all the pickers would be streaming through here on their way to the coaches. Not this morning. The yard was crawling with black-suited Home Security guards, a few police, the farm trucks were blocked in by Home Security vans in their distinctive red. A guard called out to her.

'Oi, you!'

'I've got to get to the office and...'

'No one goes anywhere unless we say so. Go and talk to the man with the laptop.'

He pointed at a young man wearing a slightly too small bomber jacket zipped up to the top. If he had been wearing a t-shirt with 'nerd' or 'geek' printed in capitals on it, it could not have been more obvious.

'Excuse me, the guard over there said I should talk to you.'

'Yes, I'm agent Foster, Steve Foster.'

Darcy tried to smile, the idiot thought he was James Bond. 'I'm a team leader here and I need to get into the office to pick up my kit for the morning. We leave for the fields at ten to.'

Agent Foster looked at his watch. Maybe she was meant to be impressed by his timekeeping.

'I see. And what's your name?' He flipped open his laptop.

'Darcy Knight. Darcy Elizabeth Knight.'

'Your mother liked Jane Austen?'

'What?'

'Your names?'

'No, I was named after a ballet dancer and the Queen. Although I guess there was that Colin Firth character in Bridget Jones. Oh, sorry he's not to be mentioned.'

Colin Firth was one of the many actors with foreign wives or husbands who had moved away, many to Hollywood. Their films were banned.

Ro looked at his wrist again. It was a useless reflex. They took his watch off him, along with his belt before they locked him in, and they had forced a new orange silicon band around his wrist. His brief flirtation with being Dylan was over. He was Dhillon with an orange arm band again.

There was no clock in the room, just a chair, a table and two piles of newspaper. He had not seen the kids since they were taken out of the van. The Child Liaison Officer, who had travelled in the back of the van with them, had been as friendly as Miss Trunchbull. She had marched them off to breakfast, when he was taken away and pushed into this room. It wasn't a cell. But then this wasn't a prison. It had been a shopping centre and now it was a transit camp whatever that meant. Transit? Where to? Whenever he listened (illegally) to the *Voice of London* (the BiG authorities had not successfully blocked radio or TV transmissions) they talked about closed borders and refugee camps. The Jungle was long gone. No one was trying to come here; the camps were full of people who had been expelled. He had seen the camps full of VNBs, people stripped of their British nationality who had been re-migrated to the continent. Re-Migration Services simply loaded trains with people and sent them through the tunnel. At first when the trains emerged in Paris and Brussels the EU border control would not let them off. The trains had backed up one behind the other, it had been winter and the stationary trains were unheated. In the end the VNBs, or refugees as they became once in Europe, had been taken off and housed in halls and community centres. Now there were refugee camps outside Brussels and Paris full not of Afghans and Syrians but Brits.

He sat up; there were footsteps outside and the sound of a key turning in the lock. The door opened. Two men walked in. One of them was wearing a bomber jacker, he was carrying a laptop. The older guy was big, thickset, his cropped hair was like a thin helmet of silver above his lean face. He looked too hard to be a copper. Middle-aged cops ran to fat. He was a soldier.

'I'm agent Norman Marshall. This is my colleague Steven Foster. We've come to ask you some questions.'

The squaddie stood over him as he spoke. It didn't feel right. He must have done it on purpose. Ro thought about getting out of the chair but that would be weird too.

'Do you mind if Agent Foster takes the chair, so he can work at the table?'

He was being too polite, too formal. Ro got up and walked round the other side of the table.

'Where are my kids?'

'I'll be asking the questions. You can see your kids after you've given me the answers.'

'Fire away.'

'It's quite simple. We want to know who helped you and how. We want to know the names and whereabouts of everyone who you met or spoke to, since you started planning to evade your re-Migration.' There was no menace in Marshall's voice, it was as calm as if he had been asking for a library book; the disinterested tone was terrifying.

'I can't tell you. I don't know the names of anyone, don't even know why they wanted to help.'

'You don't know anyone?' Marshall said with the same flat voice. 'What about Tom Smith, whose house you were found in?'

'Tom? I just know his name was Tom.' Ro felt his face flushing. He had seen this scene in countless movies. He knew all about the good cop, bad cop routine. This was different. The nerd was tapping away at the keyboard, off in his own world, and Marshall looked like he was just bored.

'Are you going to tell me what I want to know?'

'There's nothing to tell.'

'We'll have to help you remember.'

Marshall got up and went to the door. He opened it. Four guards appeared. They must have been waiting in the corridor. The other agent picked up the chair and backed it against the wall. Two of the guards picked up the table at one end, dragged it and lifted up the legs onto the piles of newspaper.

'Over here,' one of the guards told him.

He did not move.

They moved instead. All four of them, two from each side, they grabbed his arms and feet and lifted him onto the table. As he thrashed around, trying to get off and break free he noticed that Marshall had left the room and the other agent, Foster, his memory was working fine now, Foster was staring wide-eyed. They strapped his arms and legs down with nylon ties around his wrist and ankles. He was pinioned, inclined upside down on the table and he could feel the blood rushing to his head. He flexed his arms and legs; nothing. The only thing he could move was his head. Two hands clamped his head. Another pair of hands sealed his nose with cling film. He took a big breath through his open mouth. Come on, you don't need your nose to breathe, you breathe through your mouth all the time. Telling himself that didn't help, his heart was racing, his breathing too rapid. It had not taken much time to turn him from a man into a panting beast in a trap. Marshall returned.

'Thanks, I'll need one of you. You three wait outside.'

Marshall's right hand was stretched down, Ro could hear water sloshing in whatever he was carrying. Marshall raised his other hand. He was holding a see-through measuring jug; the kind Kirsty used to cook with...

Ro closed his eyes. Now he knew; he was a coward. Not a hero. Like every kid growing up he'd known that he wouldn't break. But he had broken. And broken quickly. Of course, he knew about waterboarding; he knew that it wasn't meant to drown you, just make you feel like you're drowning. He rubbed his wrists, they had burns from where he had struggled against the ties strapping him to the table. The back of his head felt tender, too much banging and twisting. What had he become?

He had collapsed in a corner of the room. As far from the table and jug as he could be. He could try drowning himself and his shame in the bucket but there wasn't enough water in there left to drown. And he knew how every muscle, every part of him would twist and fight to gulp for air. The bastards. It had not taken much. After the three guards left, the fourth had taken hold of his head like a rugby ball, that was all it took. Marshall had picked up the jug of water, grabbed his chin in his vice-like hand and asked a question, Ro shook his head and the Marshall had quietly repeated his questions, again and again, as he had poured water into his mouth.

And the truth. The truth, he had to face it, was that after ten, maybe eleven seconds, he had been willing to talk. He tried to hold his breath, to keep the water gurgling in his mouth like it were a mouthwash, but he had to breathe, he could feel the film sucking into his nostrils, and then he could not stop himself breathing and the water had poured into him. He had thought he was going to die, immediately. His body had struggled, trapped as it was, and he had sputtered and chucked up the water and then the bastard had just poured in more. And that was how it had been. He had told them about Tom (not that he knew much); about the man and the woman in Brum (Marshall asked most about them); about the large guard with tattoos; but somehow, it was like he had forgotten her, or maybe because they did not ask, he had not mentioned Darcy. He had been stupid; whenever he had got his breath back and started to calm down, he thought he could brave it out. Then they had just done it again and again. The guard constraining his head, the bored agent quietly pouring water as he repeated his questions, the other one tapping away on his keyboard. He would have saved himself a lot of bother if he had just told them everything at the beginning. Then they had left him tied up as they discussed what he had said. They were annoyed because he had no names apart from Tom. All he knew was what the others looked like. How they sounded. What they wore. Fuck. He was still shaking. He couldn't stop. It had taken less than half an hour to turn him from a man into trembling jelly, leaking water all over the floor.

Maisie grabbed Tyler and Molly's hands, clasping them tight in her own. A child in each hand. How would she be able to let go when she went back to the farm?

'Did you say goodbye to Nanna?'

'Yes. Course we did,' Tyler said.

'I'm hungry.' Molly looked up at her.

'I know, sweetie, I just thought since I'm home, we could have a treat. Give Nanna a rest. We're going to have breakfast in town.'

'I'm hungry now.'

'We'll be there in a flash.'

'Can I have a muffin or pancakes?'

'It depends where we go.' She had not reckoned on going to Costa, that was way out of her price range, and the only place with muffins. The difference between the chains and the local places was huge now.

'Mummy you're going too fast!'

Molly was nigh on running, but Maisie could not help rushing. She was desperate to get to the beach, to see for herself. She had been up for hours, waiting for the kids to wake up.

'I'll think we'll go to the café on the square,' she said as All Saints Church came into view.

'Mum, what are all those flashing lights?'

'Dunno.'

There were two police vans parked just off the round-about by the church, their blue lights blinking. Behind them the tall grey spire pointed up out of the flint flanks of the church. Maisie turned to cross the road before they got to the square.

'Oh, Mum,' Tyler said, 'can we go see what's going on?'

'Ain't you had enough of the police?'

'No, they were so nice.'

She stood, uncertain whether to cross the road and avoid whatever was going on or go and find out.

'All right. You can ask 'em.'

Tyler raced ahead.

The police vans were empty. There was a policewoman standing at the gate to the churchyard, another one down by the corner where the other gate was.

'Look, Mum! It's WPC Cotten.'

Tyler let go of her hand and ran up to the policewoman. It was the same one as the night before.

'Good morning, Tyler. How are you feeling today?'

'Mum's taking us out for breakfast as a treat.'

'That's nice. You lucky boy.'

'Good morning, say "hi", Molly.'

Molly had shrunk onto her side like a climbing plant.

'That's all right, Molly's glad to be with her mum. I can see.'

'WPC Cotten?'

'Yes, Tyler.'

'What are the police doing here?'

'Oh, not much. It's an exhumation of a foreign body.'

'What?'

'It's like they say, England is for the English, even in the graveyards.'

'Say goodbye children, we got to get that breakfast.'

The kids were happy with the fry-up. When were they ever not happy to have chips. She had scrambled eggs on toast and two mugs of tea so thick and sweet that a spoon could have stood up in it. At least that's what her nan used to say when she was a girl.

'You got any idea what the coppers are doing over by the church?'

'Yeah it was on the radio. They're exhuming that painter,' the waitress said. She was a stout, pinny-round-her-waist, no nonsense kind of woman, like Maisie's mum.

'Why?'

'He weren't verified British, was he? Not with a name like that.'

'Dante Gabriel Rossetti?'

'Yeah, he's got to be Italian.'

Her family had always lived here in Birchington-on-Sea. Her nan had always been proud of the town, proud that such a great painter would have chosen to live in the town and die there.

'He was English. His sister wrote that carol.'

'What you talking about?'

'"In the Bleak Midwinter", you know?'

'What do you mean?'

'They taught us that at school, they were right proud of the Birchington connection. We sang it every year.'

The waitress picked up her plate and the empty mug.

The kids were chasing beans around their plates with chips. There was too much for them to finish.

She picked up her phone. There it was on the NBBC Kent newsfeed.

'*Kent Police are carrying out a series of exhumations of VNBs or foreign bodies known to be polluting our graveyards. The sight of these exhumed corpses led to rumours of bodies being found elsewhere. Claims of bodies dumped on beaches are incorrect. The Commissioner said that these claims are fabricated and unhelpful. The exhumed corpses of the VNBs will be cremated and disposed of appropriately. This is part of a nationwide initiative.*'

Maisie wiped a tear from her eye. She even knew what Rossetti's grave looked like. There was a flat slab of stone with a little iron railing running round, the posts had the tops like King Charles used to have on his coat of arms, fleur de lees or something, that was English enough and then there was a huge Celtic cross in the middle. Weren't that English enough? There was even a stained-glass window in the church. The Victorians hadn't thought he was anything but one of them.

Norman sipped his coffee. He had grown up on Bond, a man of action, the kind of man he liked. Spying was not what it used to be. Steve was hunched over his laptop. There were those who had raved about George Smiley, the slow old clever spy. He was more of a Bond or Bourne type, action rather than elaborate traps. It looked like the future was Steve's – all the action a spy or detective needed now was in his fingertips. It was a shame that he had never gotten beyond two-finger typing. That didn't matter, so long as Steve and the rest like him still looked up to him, still called him boss.

'What have we got?'

He was concentrating on that dimwit Iverson. The driver had said that he had been told by one of the guards to leave the keys in the car. Now they knew which guard. Dhillon had told them. A big guy with tattoos. Steve was downloading the transcript of Iverson's interrogation.

'Ah, got it. Shall I read it out?'

'Yes.'

'Iverson, suspect, bla-de-bla, yes here it is: "Officer: Who told you to leave the keys in the ignition? Iverson: The guard? Officer: Which guard? Iverson: The guard at the gate. Officer: Can you identify him? Iverson: I don't know his name, but he was scary. Not just tall but huge and built like a shit-brickhouse. He had lots of tattoos too, they were poking up over his neckline. He said leave the keys and I fucking well did. He's not someone you'd mess with."'

Steve sat up and smiled.

'We've got him.'

'Well, not quite. We know what he looks like; big and tattooed. But that's a good lead. Get me Tess on the line.'

Steve's face flushed red.

'Come on, man up. You're going to have to speak to her sooner or later.'

Steve picked up the phone and dialled.

'Agent Marshall for Ms Webb,' Steve said.

Norman put down the phone. Tess had been business-like, he liked that, good show of professionalism and all. Steve looked down too quickly, he had been staring at him.

'So, she ran a check on who was absent the other day when we interviewed all the guards. There were two off. One Alice

Baker and one Michael White. She knew Michael White. He is big, works out and has tattoos. He's off sick today.'

Steve kept his eyes on his screen. Steve could not look him in the eye.

There was something in Tess's tone, just an edge. That was it, no more shagging her. He had better get the job done and get back up to Birmingham. They had to find the man and woman who had helped Dhillon up there.

Darcy sat on her bed in the bunkhouse. She wanted to go home, wanted to check that everyone was safe, but she was terrified that she would be followed; that they might suspect her. Think. Breathe and think it through logically, she told herself. She released the duvet from her clenched fists. Assess the facts and the risks. Fact: Maisie had rung her before the raid. Maisie knew. If Maisie knew, and they knew about Maisie, then they might have bugged Maisie's phone and then they would know she had been warned. Fact: they knew Tom was not in his house. But did they know that she and Tom were together? Did they know that Tom was at her place? Did they know she had a house? She felt sick. She wanted to go home, she wanted to hold Alfie. She wanted to feel Tom's arms around her. There were too many questions and unknowns. She couldn't. She couldn't risk leading them to him. But Ro would talk. They all talked. He knew that she was with Tom, he knew that she lived elsewhere, but he didn't know about Alfie. They would come for her soon. The best she could do was stay away.

Re-migration agents had hung around all day. One had come with farm workers on the bus to the fields. A van had followed behind and watched all day as they picked. It had been too hot to pick anything useful, the heat ruins the berries, but the pickers had stayed out longer pruning and tidying up the lines. A wasted day. It would cost Cordelia a lot in missed orders.

The thing was, what to do? Jane and Amy were sitting on their bottom bunk sharing some toast and tea. They were watching something funny on a phone, sharing the headphones. They were oblivious. It seemed like nothing penetrated their happy little bubble. She reached for her towel. A shower always helped. A shower then a walk. Walking was harmless, walking would help her think. She just could not walk in the direction of home.

Norman pulled up and parked the car in the scruffy street. It was a 1950's council estate, turned 1980's Thatcher home-owners. You could tell who had bought their homes, the ones with the extensions, loft conversions and white columns on the porch. The council ones remained uniform. It seemed that not one house, neither private nor council-owned, had been repainted in the last few years. Peeling paint and dirt was spread evenly. Like everywhere else there was a cluster of large green wheelie bins. He never had quite understood how recycling and national sovereignty were linked but one of the first laws enacted by the BiG, when the new government formed, was to end any requirement or incentive to recycle. Unused, unwanted wheelie bins huddled on most streets, often lying prostate like the abandoned homeless.

Mr White's house, number 33, was tidy. The house looked cared for, the grass was trimmed, bushy pink and blue hydrangeas bobbed in the wind. This was not what he was expecting; in his mind's eye terrorists did not live surrounded by suburban shrubbery.

'Did you check the Land Registry?'

'Yes, Gov. It's registered to a Mr Michael White.'

It was the first time Steve had called him Gov, for a while. Since before his tryst with Tess.

'Boss, remember.' Norman stared at the garden. It was not how he imagined a tattooed weight-lifter living. It was all wrong.

They waited a long time for the door to be opened after they had rung the bell. An elderly woman, wearing shapeless slacks and a checked blouse opened the door a crack. She had it on the latch.

'Mrs White?'

'Yes. Who's asking?'

'We're from BiG Home Security. We need to talk to Michael White.'

'Home Security? Is that like the police?'

'BiG Home Security was set up by the New British Government...'

Norman tugged on Steve's sleeve, Steve stopped mid-sentence. He was too young to understand; older people could not keep up with all the new government departments.

'Yes, Mrs White, we're like the police, but not.'

'Oh.'

'Do you mind if we come in and ask some questions of Mr White.'

'You can try.'

She fiddled with the lock and chain before opening the door. Then led them into the kitchen. An old man was sitting in a wheel chair, he was wearing an apron, food was dribbling from his mouth. Mrs White sat down next to him and picked up a bowl and spoon.

'Fire away. He might keep his mouth open long enough for me to get some food in him.'

'Is this Mr Michael White?'

'Obviously.'

It was moving. Two people growing old together, she feeding him like a baby, still keeping the house together, the garden maintained. She was among the best of them. It's what made it all worthwhile.

'Excuse me,' Steve broke into his reverie, 'do you recognise this man?' Steve pushed his laptop across the table to Mrs White.

The old man started rocking backwards and forward muttering in a soft moan.

'Mick. Mick. Mick.'

'Ssh, Michael. It's Mick our son. Why?'

'Does he live here?'

'Yes. We couldn't manage without him. He carries his dad up and down the stairs. There're no carers to be had anymore, not now that all them Poles and Darkies have gone. It's a blessing that he came back to live with us. He's a good boy. Works for that camp. He's one of you.'

'Is he here now?'

'No. He went on a fishing trip.'

'Fishing?'

'Oh yes, he goes fishing on his days off.' She stopped to wipe the trail of pale green soupy goo that had seeped from her husband's mouth.

'When will he be back. Tonight?'

'Oh, I don't think so. He took all his gear.'

'What do you mean?'

'He has a lot of camping equipment. A lot now that I think of it. His rods, the tent, and there were some other bags. I had to tell him to be quiet tramping up and down the stairs so he wouldn't wake his dad; he was having a nap.'

The bucket seemed a long way away. Ro pushed himself up on all fours. His left hand slapped into something wet. Vomit. That's right... he had been trying to get to the bucket before; obviously he hadn't made it. How long had he been lying on the cold floor? Gas rose up from his stomach. He burped. He could get to it this time.

He retched into the dark pail, gripping the thin plastic with each spasm; yellow bile settled in the water. The same water that they had used to suffocate him. He closed his eyes. So little water, so much pain. And then the injection. The injection had made him woozy and sick. But he had not said any more, just repeated the same things. He stood up. There was nothing left to lose. His life in England, at least, was over. They had his kids. Kirsty had betrayed him. There was nothing, not even any more bile.

'Heh! Room service!' He slammed his fist against the door. Nothing. Then he slammed it again. There was nothing better to do.

After some time, time enough for the edge of his fist to be sore and red from thudding against the door, there were voices and the sound of keys. The door opened and three Home Security Guards stepped in. Two grabbed him by the shoulders, the third yanked his hands behind his back. He felt cold metal and heard two clicks. Handcuffs. A heavy hand gripping each shoulder, the two marched him behind the guard swinging the key to the handcuffs.

'Where are you taking me?'

'You'll find out.'

They pushed him into a disabled toilet.

'Clean up.'

A faded blue towel, a set of white trunks, white t-shirt and navy overalls were piled up on the flipped down baby-changing table. No flannel, but there were paper towels. One of the guards stood in the doorway.

'Can I shut the door?'

'No. It's against policy.'

When he was ready they led him into a formal interview room with a mirror, which he assumed was a one-way window, two chairs facing each other either side of a table, a third chair by the door.

'Sit down.'

He chose the chair facing the door. And waited.

The door opened. One of the guards brought him a tray with a sad ham sandwich and glass of water on it. He was not hungry but ate; he knew his body needed fuel.

Kirsty was the last person he expected to come through the door when it opened. She looked a wreck. Her face was grey and streaked, she had been crying.

Ro sprang up. Any pity he might have felt was dwarfed by his incandescent rage. She had betrayed them.

'Don't you move.' One of the guards who had held him down during the water-boarding came in behind her. 'Back on the chair, and you, Miss, in the other one. You got five minutes.'

The guard, pulled out his truncheon as he lowered himself onto the chair by the door.

Ro forced himself to sit down. He did not take his eyes off Kirsty. She looked around the room.

'Look at me!' he said.

She pulled herself up and stared straight back at him.

'Where are the kids?'

'I'm sorry,' she spluttered and started crying, 'I'm so sorry. I got it wrong.'

'Where are they?' Ro raised his voice. 'Have you got them?'

He did not like the look of terror in her eyes as she shook her head from side to side.

'Kirsty, for God's sake, where are they?'

'They took them from me. They told me I could keep them. But they took them.'

'You idiot. We could have all been together, somewhere safe, if you...'

A strange guttural cry came out of her mouth. She lifted her hand to wipe the tears. Her wrists were bandaged. The guard paid no heed, he was checking his phone.

They had been together eleven years. They had grown up together, made babies together. He would never see her again. He knew that. If he did he would kill her. She would have to live with herself. If she could.

It had been a long day. Even so, Cordelia wondered at the wisdom of pouring herself a whisky. It was six, she could allow herself that. She did not think much of people drinking on their own, but how many times in how many movies had people reached for solace and calm in a bottle of whisky? She held it up to her lips and let the whiff of peat tickle her nose. It was a single malt from Islay. She was not much of a whisky drinker herself but kept it as a keepsake. It reminded her of Alan. Once she had given away his clothes, there had been very little of him left in the house after his death; apart from a half-finished bottle of whisky. She had even thought of giving it away. Now, she was glad she had kept it, it would cost a fortune to buy with the import duties from Scotland being what they were. She inhaled, then took a gulp. The fire sliding down her throat was surprisingly pleasant.

The best thing about living alone, without any doubt, was the mastery of the remote. She leaned into the chair, it tilted as she forced her weight back, and turned on the TV. However appealing an escape into the endless re-runs of David Attenborough series on NBBC seemed, she selected the NBBC news channel. She had to know if her little drama had made the news. It had. Of course, it had.

'...*apprehended the terrorists responsible for the attack on the Humber Bridge.*' She stopped listening and read the news flashing across the bottom of the screen. '*Kirsty Dhillon reunited with children. Runaway husband in custody.*'

She just had to wait now and there would be a report. The phone rang. She set the TV to mute.

'Hello.'

'Hi, Cordelia, it's Sandy. I hope you haven't forgotten that I'm popping by for a drink this evening.'

She had spoken to Sandy Melsom once. She had never arranged to have drinks with her. She had never given her her ex-directory home number. Nothing about today had been as expected.

'Oh, Sandy, I can't tell you how lovely that would be. It's been one hell of a day.'

'You can tell me all about it later. We can look at my wedding photos just like we planned and I can tell you about my honeymoon. Just make sure that you have a bottle of white in the fridge ready. I'll be there sevenish.'

'Do you want a bite to eat?'

'Oh, something light would be nice. Bye.'

She assumed her phone was being bugged. As did Sandy. That conversation was surreal. Her instincts told her that Sandy was not her kind of person, not someone she could trust. But she knew that Vicars was unable to meet her. Sandy knew about today.

The image of a large upside-down L-shaped metal structure silhouetted against the sky was on the TV screen. The legend *'New Gallows ready for action'* flashed up. She hit pause.

Concentrate. What words echoed. Planning, ready, and honeymoon. A honeymoon was an escape from the mundane. Sandy Melsom was coming to the rescue.

She pressed play.

'Following the new Death Penalty Act the competition was held to celebrate great British design. The winning design by Manchester-based design duo Bowles Neath captures the historic iconography of the gallows silhouette, an important part of the deterrence offered by the new punishment and combines it with the best in modern materials and engineering. Queen Catherine presented the award last year,' the picture changed to Kate dressed in a pure white suit giving a statuette to a man and a woman, *'and talked about the excellence of British design and manufacture.'*

Minus Two: Saturday

The bus seemed to take longer than ever. Maisie had got the first one at six. The return of buses was one of the few bonuses, when petrol prices sky rocketed and people stopped using cars. People had to get around – even if it was at a snail's pace.

Maisie kept on scrolling over the news feeds on her phone. There was nothing about the bodies on the beach her mum had seen. She knew now there never would be. There was a story about how the Italian had desecrated the English graveyard for too long. The bus had passed the church, Rossetti's gravestone had gone, along with his bones. She wiped a tear from her eye. In the bleak winter. Nothing was bleaker than this. What had she done?

That Dhillon guy had three kids, just like her. She had lost one. It was seeing their mother on the TV, she had looked desperate saying how she wanted her kids back, that their dad had done a runner. What if the news was fake, like really fake? Rossetti had always been a national treasure and her mum and kids had really seen bodies on the beach. Those were facts that she knew, and look at the lies on the News. What else was lies? What the fuck had she done? Those kids in Tom's house, those kids had been reading books. That meant they were being cared for. Maybe Tom and Darcy had done it outside not because they were animals but because they had nowhere else to go? Jane and Amy were always in the hut and Dhillon and his kids had been in the house... Some people didn't care, but they did. You had to respect that.

The bus turned off the main highway and started on the little road that passed behind the back of the farm. She knew it was estate land, even though it was a mixture of woods and scrub because the wall was the same one. It was a nice wall, a soft creamy stone that had gone grey and brown with age. It broke in one place, just round the next bend, where there was a little driveway. She liked the feeling of familiarity as she got close to the farm. It was not home, but it felt, had felt until yesterday, a good place to be. The bus turned the bend and Maisie glanced down the track leading who knows where. There was a person walking down the lane towards her. It was Darcy.

Darcy was nervous. She could not help it. If Ro had spilled the beans about her, Home Security would have ransacked her house by now, they would have been found out. If not, for no other reason she had to go to work so as not to draw suspicion to herself. She had wanted to get back to the farm before Maisie got back, but Maisie was already in their hut when she walked in the door. There was no sign of Jane and Amy.

'You're back.'

'Yes.' Maisie looked down.

'I wasn't sure you would be back. Not after your phone call.'

Darcy took a look outside. There was no one around. She shut the door. 'Have you any idea what you've done?'

Maisie looked at her. 'I hadn't when I rang. I think I do now.'

'What? You changed your mind? When? After you alerted Home Security, or after they came here and trashed the place and terrified everyone and took those lovely kids. You've decided now that it wasn't such a good idea after all.'

'I made a mistake. A huge bloody mistake.'

'You did.'

'It was my kids. My kids found some bodies on the beach at home. I live in Birchington, and they were out walking with me mum and they found the bodies of a man and a girl washed up on the beach.'

'Oh God. Ro and Maya.'

'No, this was last week, Thursday. It was someone else. But the point is, it wasn't reported on the news, and instead there was this whole business about digging up Rossetti. It was like a sham, a distraction, you know, fake news.'

'What are you saying?'

'I'm saying I rang the police cos I thought Tom was up to something and would get you into trouble. I wanted to protect you.'

'Protect me?'

'And then my mum found the bodies. But it was too late by then. I had already rung.'

'Protect me from Tom? You've put Tom and everyone else I love in danger.'

'It was a mistake.'

'Why should I believe you?'

'Cos when I saw those kids on the beach I thought about my Jayde.'

'Who?

'Jayde, my daughter, she's with her daddy, Jay, in St Lucia on his granddad's farm.'

'You. You've got a black daughter, a VNB, and you shopped those little kids?'

'I forget. I make myself forget about her.'

Darcy stared at Maisie. She was sitting on her bunk. She seemed thinner, could she have lost weight in two days? If you don't eat, you can. If the world gets turned upside down you can.

'Tell me. Tell me what you know.'

Jenny was not sure anymore if she hated the weekends more than the weekdays. Monday to Friday was a balancing act between the tedium of staring at the screen and typing, and the terror of getting caught bucking the system; of trying to do the right thing and lying through her teeth. Saturday and Sunday were now a hard slog and another kind of charade. Every Saturday started with her shopping, for her mother and for herself and Norman.

It was only 8:00 but the *British is Best* aisle was not empty. The loss of EU subsidies to farming had been initially devastating but in the long run, after all the trade treaties had failed to live up to their hopes, British farmers had sprung back and met the challenge. Locally grown carrots, beans, peas and spinach were being snatched up by eager shoppers under the Red Jack banner hanging above the produce. In the winter the racks were loaded with cabbage, parsnips, cauliflower, potatoes, sprouts, anything that survived the season. The neighbouring *EXOTIC* aisle was empty. Mixed salads, tomatoes, peppers, beans, peas, asparagus, courgettes, aubergines were all imported, more expensive and rarely bought. It was the same with the fruit. In the *British is Best* aisle there was an abundance of berries: raspberries, strawberries, red currants and black currants. A swarm of shoppers nudged their trolleys closer, employing that deft British manoeuvre of ramming the opposition out of the way in silence and with a poker face, pretending that nothing has happened.

The next item on her mother's list was seven bananas. A lone woman in a purple leather jacket and spray on jeans was examining the peaches and apricots in the EXOTIC aisle. The EU and the Commonwealth were their only source of non-seasonal affordable fruits. Jenny could still feed her mother's mania for mashed bananas and cream and navel oranges but not much else. The days of imported winter strawberries was long over. And now even the bananas were under threat, as the Commonwealth prevaricated between Birmingham or London being the inheritor of the previous treaty with the former UK. King Harry and London were on the ascendant in the Commonwealth, King William's choice of wife had less global currency now.

The small bananas were not too green. She counted them, there were six or five in every pack. She needed seven not ten or twelve. Jenny grabbed two small packs. She crossed them off the list. That was a challenge she never quite resolved. She could never decide whether it was quicker to shop in two rounds – once for herself and Norman and once for her mum – or to go around once with one trolley divided front and back with two lists. The shopping was like the country – one stupid, long bloody mess. She needed some chocolate.

Even sugar and sweets – the fuel of the working class for generations – had become luxury items. Previously, British factory workers had been powered by the sweet white crystals, the original product of Caribbean slavery, mixed in with tea from India, the working class living on colonial crops. Now both tea and cane sugar were subject to high tariffs, because British farms were so intent on feeding the country by planting more wheat, oats and quinoa that sugar beet production had fallen away. Chocolate was expensive and scarce.

Jenny eyed the display. Cadbury's was not what it used to be. Hershey's by another name. There was one box of Lindor truffles left. It was on offer; £25 reduced to £18. Still expensive but it would be a treat. As she reached for the red carton, a purple leather arm extended in front of hers and grabbed it.

'Last one. Beat you to it.' It was the woman from the exotic fruit aisle. Jenny glared at her. She thought of snatching it back from its cradle on top of ripe, large Italian tomatoes. The woman bared her shiny white teeth in a smile, turned and click-clacked off down the aisle in her high heels and stolen goods. The new Britain.

At the till Jenny tried hard not to lose her temper. Of course, she had ended up behind Ms Clickety-Clack who had more non-Basic Basket food than anyone else in the shop but insisted on using the app coupons for the few items that qualified from the Healthy Portions Home Makers App. Healthy Portions! The App was like re-packaged rationing. You were allowed 1500 calories per person per household per day of the Basic Basket, anything above that and the price doubled. Ms Clickety-Clack could afford the doubling easily, but still wanted her discounted prices. The scanner was having problems computing the calories per person on the Bubbly. Maybe children could not share in the booze?

An hour later Jenny slid the key to her mother's flat into the lock. The smell hit her as pushed the door in. Oh, God, she had had an accident again.

'Hi, Mum, it's me.'

She dumped the bags of shopping on the kitchen table and flicked the kettle button down. She deserved a tea.

'Mum?'

There were no signs of breakfast. Last night's washing up was still upturned in the washing rack. She could tidy it up or face the music. She was pathetic, the kitchen could wait, her mum needed her. It was hard. But harder for her mum, she had to remember. Her mum had adored Angelica and Mary Joy, the two Filipino nurses from the care home, who had worked privately with her at home after the care home had collapsed. But then their visas were rescinded, and, well, since then it had been just herself. It was hard to get any domestic help now. The new Social Cohesion and Security Act had done away with all income support and benefits – except for those over seventy and the critically disabled. The idea had been to create social cohesion by circulating the unemployed into the caring professions. Success was not the word she would have used to describe the outcome. All the work that the VNBs had carried out had to be carried out by inexperienced, untrained people.

Her mum was still in bed.

'Mum,' she said gently, 'you awake?'

She drew the curtains to let in the light. Her car was down in the resident's car park. It was the only car except for a battered red Honda Jazz that seemed to have crumpled into the ground. It hadn't been moved in years. Sunlight flooded into the room, exposing the damp patch in the corner above her mum's bed. She was still asleep. The smell was awful; she must have soiled herself during the night. Jenny opened the window. Her mum looked pale.

Jenny sat down next to her mother on the bed and knew, before she picked it up, that her hand would be cold. Thank God. This was no life. She planted a kiss on her mum's forehead. She was at peace.

What was she going to do with all those bananas?

What she did next surprised her. She pulled her phone out of her jeans pocket and dialled. It rang three times.

'Norman?'

'What's up?'

'It's my mum. She's gone.' Then the tears came. Great heaving sobs.

'I'm on my way, my love. I'll get back as quick as I can.'

She hated fucking bananas.

Norman slapped the police siren on the car. Steve loaded his bags into the boot. He was so particular, no sense of urgency. From the moment Norman had heard Jenny's cracked voice he had no thought or desire other than to get back to her. The siren was blaring before he had even pulled out of the car park.

For the first twenty minutes they drove without trying to talk. Even Steve could see that driving at speed through the weekend traffic required some concentration. Once on the motorway the siren seemed to settle into a painful throb. And then Steve started. He rehearsed everything they knew, not leaving out a single detail. He would not stop.

'The thing is we have to get Mick White.'

At last Steve stopped talking. Norman could sense him turning to check his response. He kept his eyes on the road ahead.

'We know that he took enough kit to go off grid for a long time,' Steve continued. 'We know that he was in the army. We know that he can survive.'

'What regiment was he in?' Norman had an inkling that he would know the answer.

'Well that cannot be a coincidence?' Steve said after a few moments playing with his laptop.

'What?'

'He was in the Light Dragoons.'

'Like Vicars?' Norman felt his face flushing.

'Yes,' Steve said, turning his face towards Norman again.

The suave bastard. Vicars had pulled rank and played him. That was a fail. He had had him in his grasp and let him go because of some kind of tribal loyalty. How stupid. Half the armed forces had deserted to London. Some would have stayed behind under cover.

'Look, Gov, there has to be a direct line between the strawberry farm, Mick White, Vicars and that man and woman helping them in Birmingham. We snare them and we snare the whole bloody Resistance. We're sitting on a gold mine.'

'You may be right.'

Norman slid a CD into the sound system. Oasis blasted out. He turned it up as loud as he could bear.

Three hours later Norman moved into the slip lane at Junction 4.

'Are you coming off here?'

'Looks like it.'

In the old days it would have been quicker to get into town by going around over the top, but now most of the buttresses holding up Spaghetti Junction were clad in scaffolding as emergency repairs were carried out on the concrete. A man had died last week, hit by a bit of flying concrete. They used pressurised water guns to demolish the cracked concrete but since no one bothered with the old EU or even UK Health and Safety rules anymore, well, accidents happened. Best to avoid it. The snarl-up would slow him down.

'Where do you want to be dropped?'

'I'll go home. Any bus stop.'

That surprised Norman. He thought Steve would work. His encounter with Tess must have had an impact.

Norman spent the next few minutes trying to work out how to broach the subject. There was no easy way. The Stratford Road began as a tree-lined dual carriage-way, but he had to slow down to miss the pot holes. Vacant, once modern drive-in shops with empty forecourts, boarded up Indian and Chinese restaurants and the low, solid post-war suburbia of Shirley lined the road. They were passing through Solihull when he broke the silence.

'The other night. With Tess?'

Steve looked straight ahead.

'I thought it would be good for you.'

Steve said nothing.

'You know, make a man of you?' He could feel the anger radiating off Steve.

'I don't want to talk about it.'

A few miles later, just outside the new Gallows Park, the black metal gallows squatting like a decommissioned crane in a pebble yard, Steve spoke again.

'Could you pull over here?' As soon as the car came to a stop he opened the door. 'You went too far, Gov.'

That was all he needed; a complaint or insubordination.

'Don't forget your bags.'

Norman didn't have time for this, Jenny needed him.

Steve stood in the park for a long while inspecting the gallows. He had read an interview with the designers who had talked about the elegance offered by the long carbon fibre beams, seemingly the strength weight ratio enabled them to accommodate multiple hangings on one spanning beam. The frame was forged British steel. It was like bikes, a combination of different materials; the key was the stiffness of the frame. Get the rigidity right, and it gave a little bounce; the jolt meant a faster, kinder death. Either way it was a hard fall. The press talked about the superiority of British capital punishment, none of those botched cocktails of drugs they had in the USA, or the slow-frying in faulty electric chairs. Nothing like the force of gravity, a good English force. Newton's End was the name of this prize-winning model. And it would not rust like iron, or rot like wood. The idea was permanence, as death indeed was.

Home was only five minutes' walk away. He had not wanted Norman bringing him home. He felt like he had been taken over. He had been excited to work for someone with all that experience. He just had not thought about how Norman would see through him. Of course, he had. He just had to show him what he was, what he could do. He opened the door to his flat. The array of screens spread across the desk like a welcoming smile.

It did not take long for Steve to hack into the BiG mainframe. He was going to search systematically. First, he needed to see

145

who had accessed the files relating to Dhillon and his children. He had to the cross-reference that with all the data files on those people. Pull up images for them and then trawl through all the CCTV footage on the day in question and establish who had contacted Dhillon. It was mid-afternoon, the pizza was on the way, he had work to do.

His phone rang. He looked at the name coming up. It was Tessa. It rang again. He had not seen her since the morning after and she had been all professional. Like nothing had happened. And one more time. Something had happened. Really happened. He swiped to green.

'I wasn't sure if you would answer,' Tess said.

'I nearly didn't.'

He listened to her breathing. She was nervous like him.

'I'd like to see you again,' she said.

A tight little fist of anxiety seemed to relax inside him. She, Tess, with her translucent skin, with her soft lips, and warmth. She wanted to see him again.

'Are you sure?'

'Yes. What happened between us, it's quite rare.'

He had been right, that moment when she had held her breath and her body had tremored, they had come together. They had hit the jackpot first time.

'Have you got a camera and mike?'

'Yes,' she said.

'I'll send you some links. We can talk online. It just has to be safe.'

He worked easily after his talk with her. They had had a brief chat, he had never had a woman, a real woman in his room before. He watched her intermittently all afternoon. The link he had sent her meant that he had control of her laptop and whenever it was open her camera was sending him a live stream to his screen. She knew. She was not dumb. But he had not spent too much time watching her watch Netflix. He had his own work cut out. He had checked through all the profiles of all the people who had seen Dhillon's file. There were three people who had seen it within the forty-eight hours before his failed escape. One in Re-Migration Services, and two in British Verification Department. He had trawled through their profiles and was running facial recognition software on all the traffic and security databases for that forty-eight-hour period. He would get an alarm if any one of those three individuals showed up near to Dhillon's home, place of work, or in the same video as him.

Tess was moving the laptop. Shots of white and dark, ceilings and her hands maybe. Then a dark crimson at the bottom of the screen. It was her duvet cover, he could not forget that colour. She was in the bedroom. His main PC speakers pinged, loudly. He turned away from Tess's bedroom. There was a match. Mark Cooper, a BVD official. He was walking into Dhillon's block of flats with a woman. Steve smiled. There was a good image of her. He would find a match.

There was more over-ripe and rotten fruit than Maisie had ever seen, but the weather had changed, it was overcast and cooler. They could work faster; they needed fewer breaks for water. She picked faster than ever before. Her fingers seemed to know what to do better if she was not thinking about it, like she was on automatic, like those new electric cars you saw from time to time. They were meant to be safer. Maybe that was how humans would evolve; machines would do everything for us and we could stop using our brains.

Maisie's eyes would not stay on the strawberries, even though this was her favourite variety, Malling Centenary. She kept on scanning the rows of tables as regularly as a camp guard, just to check where Darcy was. Darcy had not said much, just listened, as she had blurted out everything. Stuff she did not even know that she had thought or remembered. It was like she had re-opened this great gaping wound, all the pain of losing Jayde, all the denial.

Darcy was doing her job. Walking around checking the pickers, checking the trays, checking the boxes as they stacked up. She didn't stop moving, every time Maisie lifted her head from the berries dangling in front of her, Darcy was someplace else.

Back in the hut Maisie waited for Darcy. She took the old biscuit tin she used as a piggy bank and spilled out the coins and notes onto her bed. Amy and Jane were listening to the radio and playing cards on the top bunk. They were minding their own business as usual. She sorted the money into three piles. Old money, New money and London money. Old money was still legal tender and the coins with the Queen were still in circulation. King Charles III coins were rare and, people said, collectable. His reign had been short. The decision to reintroduce imperial measurements was meant to rationalise things and ease trade across the Atlantic. Rational? Who were they kidding? The politicians wanted to bring back some crazy old system. There had been an uproar until the Treasury had nixed the idea by costing the price of the conversion. People said that it would have been a technical nightmare; they introduced New Sterling instead. There were still 100 pennies in a pound, except you had to call them pence and they were written as a 'd' not a 'p'. And there was this useless shilling thing which was worth 5d. So, there were 20 shillings in a pound. Crazy. She carried on sorting her coins and notes, tossing them to the correct piles.

The London money had stayed the same, except Harry's face had replaced the old Queen's and Charles's. They had kept the 100 pence to a pound, but calling Harry 'Henry IX', which somehow meant Ninth, really was a bit dumb. All three currencies had been convertible for a year; they had held the three in parallel and then it had been a free fall. She would have to take her £23.43 London money to the bank one day, it was worth over £46 she reckoned.

The news came on the radio. She had started listening to the news ever since they had dug up Rossetti, ever since there had been no reports of those bodies on the beach. Would they say anything about the Dhillons?

'It was announced today that the lottery for submitting the first criminal for hanging was won by Home Security. The Prime Minister said that treason was murdering the nation. The first person sentenced to capital punishment should be someone who had betrayed us all.

The Queen opened the new Pre-Raphaelite exhibition at the National Gallery in Birmingham. The newly re-hung permanent galleries showcase the works of Edward Burne-Jones, John Everett Millais and William Holman Hunt. Queen Catherine, a former student of the History of Art, spoke about the important contribution of art to the nation.

England beat London in the One Day international at the St Johns Wood cricket ground. The disgraced London team playing at home...'

Nothing. There was nothing about the Dhillons.

The TV screen went black. Cordelia let her hand fall back into her lap. She wanted to scream. She did not. What was the point? The National Gallery had been re-hung. How could they call that miserable collection a National Gallery? She had walked through all the rooms of the real National Gallery in Trafalgar Square often enough to know how limited this collection was. But the nomenclature, the misnomer, was nothing compared to the ugliness of the air-brushing of history, the fake news. The real news item of the day was that the gallery had been re-hung without Dante Gabriel Rossetti's work. He was half-Italian, enough to get him excised from English history. She could not scream, nor throw the remote across the room because they, be it Home Security, or Re-Migration Services, were most definitely watching. She did not know if they were spying on her through her PC webcam, or her phone, or even her Smart TV, or perhaps they had installed their own snooping devices, but she was sure they were watching her.

She waited for the phone to ring. She had played Scrabble the other night with Sandy Melsom. It had been a ridiculous ruse. They had turned all the letters face up in the lid so they could see them. They spelled words out on the Scrabble board and wrote notes to each other, passing them back and forth in the dictionary. She had managed to tell Sandy that there were THREE, PEOPLE, HIDING, HELP, NEED. Sandy's last two words were: ARRANGE and EXTRACT. Under any other circumstances the use of an X without a bonus square would have been bad play. She pressed the button on the remote. There had to be something on that could distract her.

It was getting dark when the phone rang. The number showed; it was not one stored in her phone's memory, it was not one she recognised.

'Hi, it's me.' Sandy Melsom had a distinctive voice.

'Oh, hi, Sandy, how are you doing?' Did it sound as false to the spooks, as it did to her?

'I was wondering if you would like to get off the farm and have an evening out. There's that nice wine bar that serves a really good Bubbly that just opened in Tonbridge.'

'Oh, yes, I was feeling trapped.'

'Well get your togs on and I'll swing by and pick you up.'

Cordelia ran upstairs. She had to make it look for real. She changed into a pair of navy linen trousers, slipped on a silk blouse, grabbed a light cashmere cardigan and put on some lipstick.

They would need cash – Darcy wouldn't have much in the way of savings and she could not transfer her anything. Too traceable. Luckily, Alan had made her have a safe put in. When the country had crashed out of Europe there had been a big upsurge in crime, including robberies as unemployment had risen sharply, so he had taken measures. How she missed him! She could have done with his support and common sense right now.

The safe was in her clothes cupboard built into the wall. She pushed aside her smarter evening wear hanging in dry cleaner plastic to expose the lock. She tapped in the numbers and waited for the sound of the lock mechanism. The door swung open. She kept her holiday money in plastic Ziplock bags; one for the Euros, one for London. She put both in her handbag. She hesitated a second. Diamonds had crashed in value, too easy to fake, too easy to replicate. She fingered the different boxes. She levered out a red velvet box and prised open the lid, running her finger over the smooth giant pearls. Alan had bought her the pearl necklace and earrings one winter as they strolled through the Burlington Arcade. They were not white but like a burnished gold, each pearl implausibly large. He had had an ample bonus that year from his bank. She closed it and pulled out a black shiny box. She did not open it. The bangles inside came from a holiday in India, a thick, soft 22-carat gold that gleamed on her wrist when she wore them. They were too showy, she had never liked them, but they never lost value. The pearls and the gold had cost well over £20,000 at shop prices. She slipped the boxes into her handbag. She would wear the diamonds for her date with Sandy.

Steve flicked between the two images. He enlarged both. He had put his gaming monitor to work for the first time; it had the best resolution. There was no doubt. He split the screen and pulled the two windows side by side. The face on the left was of the woman accompanying Mark Cooper. The screen grab had been enlarged. The resolution was poor, fuzzy and pixelated. The face on the right was the same face. It came from government records. The facial recognition software had pulled the match up from Britishness Verification files. He would not have believed it, he would have checked for a programme mistake, except that he could see that it was the same woman. The woman accompanying Mark Cooper to warn Rohan Dhillon of his upcoming Re-Migration was Jennifer Melissa Marshall née Chartridge, Britishness Verification Department Official, married to Norman Thomas Marshall, Home Security Agent.

Steve sat back in his chair. Norman Marshall's wife was working in the Resistance. She was undercover, right in front of them, hiding in plain sight; text book practice. Did Marshall know? Was he in on it? Steve's eyes wandered to the left-hand screen; Candyxxx15 was gone, Tess was staring ahead, reading something online. She would not believe it: Marshall's wife! What should he do? Go to Marshall or Rick McPherson? He could shop him. Tess's focus changed. She had finished what she was reading. She looked at the screen openly.

'Are you there?'

Steve stared at her. There she was: a real woman. A woman that he had had, that he could remember the smell of, a woman who wanted him.

'Steve?'

He clicked a button with his mouse and turned his mike on.

'Yeah.'

'You still working?'

'Yes, I've had a breakthrough, there's just something to resolve.'

'I was thinking – tomorrow being Sunday – would you like me to drive up?'

He stared at the screen. It was real. She wanted to drive hours on her own to come and see him. He clicked another button, turning his video on.

She smiled.

'When?' he said.

'Now.'

He looked around his room. 'I don't get many visitors. My place is not exactly tidy or nice like yours.'

'Is there a bed?'

'Yes.'

'We'll be fine then. I think we should get to know each other a bit better.'

He had about four hours before Tess got here. He had to tidy up. He was out of bin bags and cleaning stuff and had to go and buy some, and some milk, biscuits and two ready meals: chicken in wine with bacon and mushrooms. It looked like *coq au vin* but there was no way of calling it that now. He had piled in two red wines, stopped short of Bubbly, but went back to get some chocolate. Women liked sweet things. He had filled two bin bags with cans, bottles, take away boxes before he reached a decision.

He swiped right over Norman's number. Without Norman having pushed him, there would be no Tess coming to see him now. He owed him.

'Yes, this better be good. My wife has just lost her mother.'

'I know, boss. This is about her. I can't talk now, not over the phone, but can you come over to my place? I would not ask but I promise you it will be worth your while.'

'About Jenny?'

'Yes.'

'At your place?'

'Yes, sorry, I'm all set up here, and I don't have time to get to the office and back in time for... well, Tess will be here in a few hours.'

Norman parked his car outside the address that Steve had given. It was the ground floor flat of a 1930s' brick semi-detached house. There were three bin bags in the front garden, there was no water on them from the morning's shower, they had just been dumped. Steve was a bona fide cliché; geek, computer nerd and porn addict living on beer and pizza if the bag contents were anything to go by. And now Tess was coming to see him. Norman felt like a god-father to them. At least he'd never have to play with those ridiculous toys again.

When he had got back that morning and Jenny had flung herself into his arms, he'd had one of those moments when he realised, or relived, or re-woke, it was not clear what it was, but he felt his love for her burning fiercely. Mostly these days love was not in question, it was habit and duty, but sometimes she would do something, or say something which either made him see the girl he had been besotted with, or made him feel like the boy who had fallen so hard in love. Maybe it was the tears, maybe it was her vulnerability, but today was one of those days when their passion had re-ignited. It was luck that he had got out of bed to go to the loo when Steve had rung. The phone was only on vibrate. Now he was here. It had better be good, he'd left Jenny sleeping under their warm duvet.

Norman rang the bell, he did not wait long. Steve was holding a brand new yellow duster when he opened the door. The cloth still had the ironed creases in it, although one side was dark with dirt.

'We have a situation.' Steve said. It was like he learned his lines from films. He stepped back from the door. 'You had better come in.'

The room was as Norman had expected, except it was tidy. Two desks covered with a jumble of wires and gizmos and three huge screens. The screens were subdivided into smaller virtual screens. The news was streaming on the right screen, the large middle screen was blank, and the left-hand screen was logged into Home Security. Steve sat down and picked up the mouse. The room was dominated by the huge poster of a silver haired warrior queen carrying baby dragons hanging above the bed.

'So, boss,' Steve had dropped the Gov, Norman was in favour again. 'I trawled through all the video footage and found the identity of the man and woman who warned Rohan Dhillon. Before I show you, I just wanted you to know that I have not told anyone else yet. I thought you would want to be fully informed of the next move.'

The screen on the left was asleep, an expanse of black.

'Thanks, fine. Who are they?'

Steve shook the mouse. The screen woke up. Three windows appeared on the screen, three images: a shot of a man and woman, a head shot of Mark Cooper, and the official ID portrait of Jenny. Jenny and Mark were the man and the woman.

'Are you sure?' Norman felt winded. He gripped the desk with both hands and leaned forward, staring closely at the pictures.

'Incontrovertible,' Steve said. 'Cameras tracked them all the way to Dhillon's block of flats, at the right time. Although there are no images of them knocking on his door.'

'Can I sit down?'

This changed everything.

Norman ignored Steve looking at his watch. They had been at it for two hours but he needed just one or two more things. Patience. The later he left the more he would know, the more control he would have. He had made Steve show him how to install spyware on Jenny's computer. They had practised three or four times on Steve's. Steve had shown him all the footage, all the footprints of Jenny and Mark going to Dhillon. He logged every page, every link.

'I think we're done. Tess will be here soon.' Steve said.

'Can't you track her?'

'Who? Your wife?'

'No, Tess.' Norman forced himself not to snap. 'Then we could see how much time we've got.'

Steve opened his mouth to protest. Norman met his stare. Then Steve unlocked his phone.

'And show me how you do it. I'll track Jenny's phone.' Norman got out his own phone and turned the video camera on. 'What are you doing?'

'I'm not as young or as savvy as you. If I video what you're doing I'll be able to remember how you did it.'

Steve stared at him for a second then his attention returned to the screens. 'She's just coming off the motorway.'

'Is there anything else I need to know?'

'No, don't think so. You've got all the links, the footage and the photos. You know how to install the spy-ware. You've got what you need.'

Steve shoved his phone back into his pocket. He dragged his wallet across the desk and snatched it up. He was like a hare about to bolt.

'Sure. I'll get the surveillance all set up today. She'll be busy with the funeral arrangements.' Norman changed his tone. 'You probably want to get that wine open and the table laid; women like that kind of thing.'

He looked around the room.

'You have got flowers for her, Steve?'

'Flowers?'

'Of course.' Norman looked at his watch. 'You've got time. For God's sake don't mess this up.'

'I can't find my keys,' Steve's voice was tight.

'They were on the desk!'

Steve got on his knees and started rummaging around the piles of paper and magazines.

'Look, you go. I'll look for them while you get the flowers. I'm in no rush to see Jenny.'

Steve nodded. He was in a panic.

'Go!'

'Thanks, boss,' Steve shouted over his shoulder before he slammed the door.

Jenny had no idea how long Norman had been talking. Her hand was still on the mug of tea but she had not picked it up once while he was speaking. It was still warm. Time had slowed down as her mind raced. He knew that she and Mark had approached Rohan Dhillon, he knew that Mark had arranged the pick-up, he knew that she was knee deep in the Resistance, that she was culpable. But he was sitting next to her, looking at his PC screen, their legs rubbing alongside each other. On the monitor in front of them was the fuzzy screen grab of her and Mark.

There was no point trying to make a run, or fight him. She knew how fast and agile he was; when they were just playing in bed he could hold her down lazily with one arm. She did not know what to say. She lifted the tea to her mouth.

'It's still hot.'

He took up his mug too. They drank staring blindly at the screen.

'I never thought you would be the one to find out.'

'That was luck.'

'I can't deny it. And I'm not sorry. I've helped a lot of people.'

'When did you start?'

'It was Debs. She asked me to help with Hakim, Sami and Yasmin. For Chrissakes, they were my nephew and niece. It all changed for me then. I tried, I tried so hard, but it made no difference, I failed. After the sinking, I realised it was not just my family who needed help. That I had a duty. Debs's suicide just made me more determined.'

'But what about me?'

'I knew you would not budge. You're too much a soldier.'

'You're right.'

'Norm, I didn't think about it. I couldn't. This was something I had to do. But I stayed with you.'

'Why?'

Jenny looked down at her bare feet. She was naked under her dressing gown; he had asked her to get up quickly. She had assumed it would be about her mother.

'I stayed despite your stupid bloody politics because you are loyal and I love you. I lost my family, I didn't want to lose you too. I just couldn't tell you about this,' she pointed at the screen.

'Didn't you trust me?'

'I trust you to do the right thing. That's the way you are, Norm; you follow orders, you run down tram lines. You're safe and predictable. And I love you for it.'

'I am.'

'Could I ask just one thing. Let me get my mum buried before you turn me in. I won't run. There's no point. Here, you can have my phone.'

She pushed her phone over the desk towards him.

'You're forgetting one thing.' He clamped his hand over hers. 'I am loyal to what I love.'

It did not take long for Jenny to isolate all the security footage that Steve had found of Mark and herself, and two more from cameras that he had missed. Norman had noted down everything meticulously, taking photos of all the relevant web pages and links. Jenny's training with the Resistance had been in software. She knew not only how to cover her tracks, but how to make evidence disappear and if necessary doctor it.

'You've been hacking into my accounts all the time,' Norman said as he put a new mug of tea on the desk.

'You're shockingly lax; I mean, your passwords? To think you work in security!'

She tilted her head up to him, he kissed her.

She felt a bit giddy. This was the first thing that they had really done together in ages. Perhaps being found out was the best thing that could have happened.

'We have to make a choice now. I can just delete every image and video from all the records and cover my tracks as best as I can. Or I can corrupt the images; make them unrecognisable.'

'Or put Steve's face on?'

'What? It'll be enough just to remove the evidence that it was me. Surely? He wouldn't go up against you and say you had turned. Not you, not with your record.'

'It's too risky. The only way to keep you safe is to play the move. Not only does the evidence incriminating you have to go, we have to incriminate him. I've got an idea; I think it'll work.'

'It's a treasonable offence.' Jenny watched her husband's face. He was looking at the screen impassively.

'I know. I don't want to see you hang.'

All those other women, all those slags, all his stupid politics, but when it came to it, this is what he was. He put his hand in his trouser pocket and pulled out a small set of keys attached to a ring with a three-headed dragon in a circle of silver.

'Whose are those?'

'Steve's. I've got a plan. But it will only work if you incriminate him. And I need you to activate this link.'

He scrolled through his emails.

She looked at the email. It was an invitation from Steve to take over his PC.

'Not bad, Norman. Is it active?'

'If we are lucky.'

'How did you do this?'

'I played stupid. I kept on getting him to show me how to set it up here so I could snoop on you, did it so many times that the last time he was distracted by Tess coming.'

'Tess. Tess from Ashford?'

For a second, she felt a wave of jealousy, but it passed. There was nothing to forgive.

'Yeah. They're a thing now. Anyway, I think he forget to un-install it the last time and then I swiped his keys. We should be able to watch him. And I've got this plan. You get to it, I've got some calls to make.'

Although the TV was on, Norman was not holding the remote. Jenny had set up the link to Steve's computer on her laptop and then mirrored it so they could see and hear better on the big screen and speakers.

They were watching Steve's buttocks moving up and down on the bed. Norman guessed it was not by accident that furniture was arranged so that the webcam had a good view of the bed from Steve's desk. After watching Steve and Tess eat they had turned the sound off.

'I almost feel sorry for him.' Jenny said, looking away from the oscillating white bottom.

'He's a nerd. I don't think he had even met a real woman in the flesh until I got them together.'

Steve's buttocks shuddered. He stopped moving, then rolled off.

'Turn the sound up. Post-coital talk is the time for secrets.'

Norman picked up the remote and switched on the sound as Steve pushed the pillows against the wall and leaned back into them. The ash-blonde warrior queen on Steve's poster stared past them.

'What was this thing that you were working on today?' Tess said, pulling herself up and leaning into Steve's chest.

'The thing is,' Steve put his arm around her, 'Norman thinks he's good at his job, so dedicated, but can't see under his own nose.'

'What do you mean?' Tess said, trailing her finger around his mouth.

'She's not done; she'll want him to tie her up soon. I better get going,' Norman said.

'Shh,' Jenny said.

'Well,' Steve continued, 'it's highly confidential, top secret and all but it looks like his wife is implicated in the Dhillon business.'

'No way. Tell me.'

'I'm going around there now,' Norman stood up.

'Are you sure he'll tie her up?' Jenny asked.

'I'm certain. I know that look.'

'Did you?' There was an odd expression in Jenny's eyes, hurt and a little frightened too.

'It's not my thing,' he kissed her, 'you are.'

'Be careful.'

'Keep recording until I get there. Just make sure that whatever we leave behind incriminates him.'

Norman sat in his car watching Steve and Tess on his phone. Steve was nervous. Tess urged him to relax and gave him a tumbler of whisky. It took him a long time to tie her up securely enough. Tess kept on urging 'tighter, tighter.' Steve really did not get it. Finally, she was trussed and secure. Then Steve had mounted her and Norman had to endure a few minutes of Steve's bobbing arse again. She must have said something then because the boy-wonder rifled through her bag and until he pulled out the black silk cord.

'Is this the one?' Steve asked.

Tess's answer was not audible but Norman knew what the cord was for. He jumped out of the car, and sped around the corner into Steve's front garden. He did not give much hope of Steve continuing for long but timing was crucial. He watched on his phone. Steve had bound the rope around her neck and was pulling hard. He stopped. Norman put on the disposable gloves he had taken from where Jenny kept them under the kitchen sink. Steve pulled and released again.

Norman was in the lobby. Steve yanked the cord, Tess writhed for a few seconds. Steve stopped. Steve pulled the cord again, he held it a little longer as Tess struggled. The next time Steve managed a bit longer. A message from Jenny flashed over his screen.

'That's enough. Go.'

Norman slid the key into Steve's lock. Steve was tightening the cord again. Norman turned the key. Steve was counting aloud. He just did not get it. Steve released the rope. Norman pushed the door open.

'What the fuck?' Steve said.

'Hi, hi, Tess. Sorry to barge in, but I found the keys, and thought I had better bring them back.'

'I think you should leave. Now.'

Tess was shaking her head, her mouth sealed by the thick pink tape. The black silk cord fell from Steve's hand as he pointed at the door, his other was clamped over his crotch. Steve was never going to take him on.

'I don't think so,' Norman said as he walked over to the kitchenette.

'Look,' he picked up the whisky bottle. 'We need to talk, about my wife.' He poured two tumblerfuls. His back was to the bed, he extracted the paper tissue from his pocket and put it on the work top. It unfurled to reveal two tiny paper envelopes. He picked up one and carefully upended the crushed Rohypnol into one of the glasses. He gave it a shake then took a sip from the other.

'Here, drink this.'

Steve had not moved. He was like one of those living statue acts they used to get on the South Bank in London. Maybe they still did. People had become desperate to earn a living there, so they said.

'Now.'

Steve took the whisky.

'You see – no offence, Tess – but I've realised that I love my wife.'

'Does that mean you're not going to turn her in?' Steve said.

'Exactly.'

'But... but,' Steve creased his eyebrows together, as if he were calculating the ramifications.

'But,' Norman finished Steve's sentence, 'protecting her would be treason and it would implicate me.'

'But I've got all the evidence.'

'So, you would report it?'

'I would have to.'

'That's what I thought. Sit down.'

Norman took the glass from Steve and re-filled it, taking his time to empty the second sachet of ground *Rohypnol* and shake it until it dissolved. Steve hunched forward, burying his head in his hands. Thinking would not help him. Norman nudged the glass against Steve's fingers.

'Cheers,' Norman raised his glass.

Steve looked at his.

'Drink up!'

Steve downed his again. 'Are you going to turn yourself in?'

'No, I thought you might be able to help me. That's why I came around.'

'How? By giving you some time to get away?' Steve looked hopeful.

'No. I just need to wipe some stuff from your PC.'

'You can't.'

Norman pulled out his gun.

'I can. You go and lie next to Tess, she's cold. Look, she's shivering. Keep her warm. Don't take off the tape off. I'm in no mood for an earful right now.'

Steve climbed over Tess's prone body and lay down next to her. Norman reckoned that he would have to wait about ten more minutes before the drugs worked. He pulled out the paper that Jenny had scrawled the instructions on. He had to wait for her go. She would be playing with Steve's PC. The plan had been to stitch the footage of him strangling Tess together so that he looked like he had killed her. They needed at least thirty seconds, a minute would be better.

'Steve, are you awake?'

'Yes.'

He glanced at his phone. Jenny would text instructions. Nothing. He swiped from screen to screen. He thought about playing Tetris; he checked his emails.

'*Is he asleep?*' Jenny's text flashed across the top of the screen.

'Steve?' Norman said.

There was no reply.

'Steve!'

Silence.

'*I'm ready,*' Jenny texted.

He closed the webcam. Jenny did not need to see this, and it would save having to wipe the record afterwards. Steve was breathing deeply. He was lying on his side up against Tess's crucified body. Norman poked him. No response. He went to Tess's side of the bed, stuffed the gun down his trousers. She was not shivering but trembling, her eyes were wide with panic. She was brighter than Steve.

'I'm sorry,' he said, as he took up the black silk cord and wound one end round each hand. He closed his eyes rather than look into hers as he yanked his hands apart.

Minus One: Sunday

Cordelia leaned heavily against the police station door. It did not budge. She pushed the buzzer again. She could see the reception inside; there was no one behind the desk. *Buzz. Buzz.* There were two men slumped in chairs along the wall. They seemed to be asleep. *Buzz. Buzz.* She kept her finger pressed onto the round plastic button. There was a click and a whirr, the door opened inwards.

'Come on,' she said, stepping in.

Sandy came close on her heels. The bruise around her eye was beginning to discolour. She had blood smudged round her mouth. Cordelia wondered if she looked as bad.

A door opened behind the desk, a tired-looking woman came out. She moved towards them with no urgency and found some stuff to shuffle around the desk before she seemed to notice them. She put her fingers on the keyboard turning her eyes to a screen.

'Hello, can I help you.'

'Yes, my name is Cordelia Hughes and this is Sandy Melsome. We would like to report a crime?'

'Are you VB?'

'Yes.'

'Can I see your ID card.'

'It was stolen.'

The woman stared at Cordelia. 'Wait a minute.'

She walked round to another desk and opened a drawer. She returned with a thick tablet. She put it on the counter.

'Right hand on here. Please.'

Cordelia put her hand on the fingerprint reader. The screen flashed. A British Verification Department logo appeared. The tablet emitted a low chime.

'You can take your hand off now.' The woman took the tablet back. She looked at the screen and back at Cordelia, then read out from it.

'Cordelia Jayne Hughes, born 6th March 1969?'

'Yes.'

'And what did you say the crime was?'

Cordelia wiped her face with a tissue; it came off stained with dark red. She looked at the desk officer.

'Assault and theft.'

'What was stolen?'

'My bag, my wallet, my jewellery, our phones. Her car, her bag, her wallet, her jewellery, '

'Was force or the threat of violence used?'

'Yes.'

'Robbery, then.'

'What?'

'I'm putting down robbery. Could you fill in these forms, return them to me and then wait here until you are called and a statement is taken.'

They had waited an hour before they were called into the interview rooms. One at a time. Cordelia concentrated on remembering the details. Two guys, who were parking as she and Sandy arrived, had tried to move in on them. They had eyed them up from the bar before sauntering over and breaking into their conversation. Sandy had made out that she was drunker than she was and had stood up and shouted at the men to leave them in peace. Then she had sat down and told Cordelia to remember everything about them.

The sergeant taking the statement from her yawned.

'And could you describe the assailants?'

'Yes, there were two of them. They were about forty. One was about five ten, the other, maybe six foot, he was taller but not too tall. The shorter one was thin, the tall one was heavy.'

'Which one punched you, Mrs Hughes?'

'The shorter one.' He had been the more persistent of the two, he had offered her every drink under the sun, but would not leave her alone.

'What did he look like?'

Cordelia had never been one for lying. And never against the authorities, against the law. Not until she had started keeping a false set of accounts to protect her workers, like her father before her. Now she had no qualms about lying. Sandy said that by making a scene, there would be lots of witnesses who could corroborate their claim that the men had been hassling them. It was all about plausible memories however false they were.

'He was wearing an orange t-shirt. It was a Rolling Stones one. Jeans. Trainers with orange laces.'

'Did you notice anything else?'

'Yes, his hair was short, probably disguising baldness, you know the look.'

The sergeant looked at her, his pen poised.

'I didn't notice his eyes. But he had bad teeth.'

Cordelia waited for Sandy with two drunk men and an old couple. It was just after two when Sandy emerged. She had cleaned the blood off her face but her eye was beginning to close from the swelling. Before she sat down next to Cordelia she returned to the desk.

'Excuse me, constable, but could you ring for a taxi for us? We don't have any money now to get home.'

They did not talk, not until they got into the taxi.

'Did you remember what they looked like?'

'Yes,' Sandy said, 'I'm proud of myself. I even remembered their number plate. They arrived at the same time as us. I clocked it then, luckily.'

'They'll be able to find them?'

'Yes, and that's where they will look for my car. They'll go straight to the registered address and meanwhile they won't be looking for it on the open road.'

Cordelia grabbed Sandy's hand and squeezed it.

'Getting that giant to punch you was brave but mad.'

'Clever, wasn't it?' Sandy said, brushing her fingers over her bruised face.

'We did it!'

Cordelia felt a surge of jubilation. Time was the only thing they could offer Tom and Darcy now.

Ro was dead to the world when the door opened. He had not heard the key turning in the lock. It was the sound of boots and the door swinging against the wall that woke him. The light was blinding. Two guards were in the room, another stepped in.

Ro had not seen daylight since they had raided the house and they had bundled him into the waiting vans. That was only yesterday morning. They had come Friday at dawn. No clocks, just windowless cells and harsh lighting but he had heard the guards changing over when they brought him food. It must be sometime Saturday night or Sunday morning. Two days and he had already lost his sense of time.

'Out you come.'

There was no point resisting, that just got him a beating. He had learned that lesson. Just go with the flow. They did not take him to the room where they had tortured him. They turned left this time, down another corridor with doors blank except for the uniformly high peep holes. He guessed it was late, the guards were not bothering to banter and joke, they were quiet. Their boots thudded heavily on the floor, as his bare feet slapped against the cold. Trainers had laces, and they had been taken those off him right at the start.

They came into a canteen. Long tables with eight chairs apiece spread in orderly rows across the room. Three female guards were standing over someone sitting on the middle table at the far end under a clock, it was 02:23. The guards pushed him towards the clock.

'Daddy!' Maya jumped up and started to move towards him. He wanted to run to them, the guards grabbed him from behind.

'Stay here.'

Neel was sitting on Kiran's lap. Neel started crying. As he got closer he could see how hard Kiran was holding back his tears. Ro was proud of him. The guards let them all go once he had got to the table. He kneeled down as they flew into his arms.

'Oh, I've missed you.'

He stood up as Neel and Maya clung to his legs, crying. Kiran held back. Ro reached over and pulled him into a hug.

'Thank you, Kiran, I can see you looked after them.'

'They should finish their drinks,' one of the guards said. 'There won't be any drinks or snacks on the journey.'

They were in a van again. The female guards had given them a sweet each as they loaded up. One of them had even kissed the kids goodbye. Maybe they weren't all bad. They drove for about an hour. Neel fell asleep on his lap, Maya slumped into his side. Even Kiran slept.

The van came to a halt. The driver's door slammed. There were footsteps coming towards them. Ro had assumed that they were being taken to Ashford to continue their interrupted journey. He was surprised to see nothing. It was very dark outside when the van door opened.

The children were out of it, he could not rouse them. Six guards wearing black uniforms appeared. Two helped him carry the kids out of the van. They were in the countryside somewhere, all he could see in the car lights was the road stretching out ahead, lights lined it into the distance. He followed the men carrying Maya and Kiran round to the front of the van. There was a small plane about 100 meters ahead. This was not a road it was a runway. Kiran opened his eyes.

'Are we going on the plane?' Kiran asked.

The man set him down.

'I don't know. It looks like it.'

'Where are we going?'

'To France or Holland, I guess.' The Dutch were more receptive than the Belgians to the re-migrants, France was bigger and could take more.

The other guards stood on either side of the stairs leading up to the plane. Like an honour guard, Ro thought as he followed the guard carrying Maya up the steps. Kiran's hand was resting on his arm. It looked like a military plane from inside, at least not a passenger one. Maya murmured as the guard put her down on a bench running down one side. He strapped a belt over her. Kiran sat down and strapped himself in.

'And the little one here,' the guard ordered. Neel did not wake up. There were ropes, harnesses and large bags stashed under the benches. The guards followed onto the plane. How could they be worried about what the children might do? There was no escape now, whatever happened. One of the guards rolled a shutter down. It was transparent door. Ro could see the dark outside.

The take-off was bumpy but the plane climbed quickly. They flew over a big town, Canterbury perhaps, and over fields and roads and then he could see the necklace of lights along the coastal road. Then the inky blackness of the sea.

As soon as the plane began to level off, the guards undid their belts. They fiddled with some clamps and wires attached to the side of the galley.

'Could you get up, we need you to sign some papers,' one said, waving a form.

Ro found it hard to unbuckle himself. The guards were not looking at him. He got up unsteadily. The plane was banking round. He took two steps. The guards swarmed and surrounded him, they pulled his arms behind his back and clamped them together. They bound his wrists with something tight – a plastic tie digging in. They held him close. He could hear their fast breathing by his ears. One of the guards moved off to the shutter door. The man bent over and heaved the door up and open. The cold wind rushed in. Ro understood.

'Daddy!' Kiran cried.

'Not the kids,' he screamed as they dragged him to the gaping hole, 'Not the children, please...'

Darcy was usually a deep sleeper. She was exhausted but she could not sleep. She knew that Tom was awake too, his breathing was too loud. Three days ago, her life had been routine. Falling in love with Tomasz, having him here in her bed, would normally have been momentous. It was nothing now, nothing compared to the fear, the sheer panic that he would be found, that his trail would lead them to discover Alfie. Yet, she could no more turn Tomasz out then cut off her own limb. She rolled onto her side and wrapped her arm over his chest.

'Can't sleep,' she said.

'I know.'

'I'm scared.'

'We would be stupid not to be,' he said.

Perhaps they dozed. She was not sure. Her heart was pounding and she was sitting up in bed before she understood that someone was thumping on the front door. Tom was already at the window.

'It's a Range Rover. Unmarked. Could be secret ops?'

'Get under the bed. They can't be here for you.' Darcy stumbled in her panic to get dressed. She was still pulling a t-shirt down over her head when she collided with her mother on the landing.

'Keep Alfie quiet.'

She rushed downstairs.

'I'm coming,' she said as she approached and turned the hall light on.

The hammering on the door stopped.

She took a deep breath and opened it. A huge man, with buzz-cut hair, and muscled arms covered in tattoos was standing in front of her.

'You must be Darcy Knight? You had better let me in.'

'Why? Who are you? What do you want?'

'You've got Tom Lisek here and Alfie Knight?'

'Who sent you?'

'I don't know her name. We don't use names. But the lady who told me to come here gave me these to give to you.'

He thrust a large envelope towards her. There was a note scrawled across the front. *For Darcy. To help you on your way.* She recognised the handwriting. It was Cordelia's. There were two bags of money and two jewellery boxes inside.

It had been gone two thirty when the tattooed man arrived, he gave them fifteen minutes to pack. Take essentials, one suitcase each, he'd said. Darcy stuffed her bag; what do you take when you don't know where you are going and for how long. Her mum sorted out Alfie's things. Tom did not have much. Just what he was wearing and a change of clothes. Darcy filled a second case. Tom could take it for her. He'd gone downstairs to make the big man a strong coffee with two sugars. They were not talking.

When they were ready Darcy scooped Alfie out of bed, wrapped him in a blanket, hugged her mother and climbed into the back of the car. She lay Alfie down and hooked the safety belt over him while Tom and the tattooed man hefted the bags into the boot.

The engine turned on and the man backed the car down the lane. He reversed into the main road so that he was facing away from the farm.

'Is this the way to the A20?' he asked.

'Yes.'

'What's the deal?' Tom said.

'I drive. We don't get stopped. There'll be a handover before the M25. We'll get a call or text with the location. They get you into London.'

'Whose car is this?' Darcy had never sat on cream leather seats before.

'Again, I don't ask for names. But as far as the police are concerned this car was hijacked from the friend of your lady friend. A good looking blonde woman.'

Cordelia could not be described as a blonde, her brown hair had long since faded to dark grey.

'My lady friend? You mean the one who gave me the envelope?'

'Yes.'

It came to Darcy; it had to be the woman that Cordelia had met at the National Farmers' do on Wednesday. Cordelia had told her about Sandy Melsom turning up for a 'drink' the night after the raid. She was quite a local celebrity, there were often pictures of her in the local newspaper. She was a blonde.

'Expensive looking?'

'Yeah. Reeks of money.'

'So, they are going to be coming after you? The police?' Tom said.

'No,' the tattooed man told him, 'she said they would get the police looking in the wrong direction. Give a false report.'

Darcy looked out of the window at the barely visible dark fields. So many people were caught up in this, helping them or hindering them or just collateral damage. Cordelia had given her a small fortune in jewellery, and Sandy Melsom had given up her car. And they had never even met.

'Will she get it back?'

'It'll be insured,' the tattooed man said.

Maisie woke up in the middle of the night hungry. Amy and Jane were asleep. Darcy's bunk was empty. She had waited all afternoon, all evening, she had not even dared to leave to make supper. Now her stomach was rumbling. Darcy was not coming back. She picked up the bags of Old and London money and stuffed them in her jacket pocket. There was only one thing to do; she started to walk, retracing the route that the bus had taken the morning before. That's where Darcy would be. Up that lane. Maisie pushed herself into the hedgerow as she saw the lights flashing ahead and heard a car coming along the bus route. It turned off the road, at the same turning she was heading to. Who would be driving around at this hour?

Why had she even come? It was gone two. She couldn't wake Darcy up and hand her the money at two in the morning. Did she intend to leave it on the doorstep? It was barmy. Yet her feet carried her forward along the road to the gap in the wall. It was silent. The car had cut out. She was sure Darcy was in trouble. Maybe she could help.

She stumbled a few times, the track was unpaved and uneven, little rocks stuck up here and there. The path turned away from the road, snaking round again so when she finally came on a clearing with the SUV and a little house she was surprised. She had never seen it from the road. It was a good place to hide out. What did Darcy have to conceal? The house lights were on. The SUV was dark. She approached it. It was empty. She thought about going around the house and looking in through the windows. But settled on waiting outside. Last time she had looked in through Tom's windows it had only caused trouble. There was a barn off to the right of the yard, she hid herself down the side of it. She could peep around the corner and watch what happened.

The door opened and the silhouette of a giant blocked the light. The man came out carrying a bag, there was another smaller man with him. They stuffed the bags in the boot. Darcy came out carrying a child, an old woman embraced her and then she climbed into the back of the car with the child. The two men got into the front of the car. The doors slammed shut, the engine turned on, the lights dazzled her and then they were gone. The sobs of the old woman standing on the doorstep watching them disappear into the night pierced her. She had done this. Maisie had had no idea Darcy had a child and now they had them both. This was on her.

After a while the woman stepped back into the house. She turned all the lights off downstairs. One by one she turned the top floor lights off until there was only one left on. Maisie hugged herself against the cold and waited until the last window went dark. She walked back to the farm, packed her bag and went back out. She was going to catch the first bus home. She had to be with her kids. She needed Molly and Tyler in her arms.

The irony did not escape Darcy. She could not remember the number of times they had picked people up at Ashford and handed them over to someone else at a specific GPS point. She knew the routine and now they were the freight.

After they had set off, the big man had received a text with GPS coordinates. He drove to a narrow street on the edge of a village lined with empty dark cars. He pulled up just beyond the last street lamp. The houses petered out and the road vanished into the dark of a country lane ahead. It was quiet. Darcy bit her nails, she knew she had been anxious ever since the raid but now sitting here waiting she was terrified. She reached over the car seat and rested her hand on Tom's shoulder. His hand fastened onto hers; they were in this together.

'How long will you wait?' Tom said.

'I was two minutes early. I'll give them another three.'

'What happens if they don't come?'

'I'll take you but there is a danger that the police will be looking for this registration number by now.'

'What's the time?'

Darcy closed her eyes and counted to sixty. She opened her eyes; nothing. She closed them again; one, two, three... was this the end of the road?

'I have an idea,' Tom said.

'What?' The tattooed man turned to look at Tom.

Tom opened the glove compartment.

'If she's got any tools I'll swap number plates with one of the cars on the street.' Tom bent forward, the tattooed man watched for a moment.

'It won't work,' he said, 'the border works on automatic number plate recognition. It'll clock the mismatch between car and number plate. It'd be like waving a red flag at a bull.'

'That means we can't get in to London in this?' Darcy said.

'Not a chance.'

'What if they don't come?'

'We'll worry about that in a minute.'

They did come. Or rather a young man came in a van, Copstone Farm was just visible on its back doors. It made sense: London was the biggest market for all the farmers. Everyday trucks and vans poured into London bringing food from New Britain. Every day, thousands of people with visas and BiG approval traded back and forth. The van parked on the dark end of the lane. It flashed its lights three times. The tattooed man flashed back twice. Both drivers got out. They met between the cars and then Tom's door opened.

'It's okay. He's your ride into London.'

The door by Darcy opened too. The young man peered in. Three earrings glinted in the faint lamplight.

'Best he stays asleep. Can you get out or do you need help?'

In less than a minute they were sitting on their suitcases behind stacked boxes, concealed just as they had hidden the Dhillon family when they had rescued them from Ashford camp. Darcy sat next to Tom and leaned into him, Alfie barely stirred.

'We'll be all right,' Tom said, kissing her head.

It was no more than a thought, no more than a hope, but it is what she needed. All they could do was sit tight and hope that they were not stopped.

'Good luck,' the tattooed giant said as he swung the van door shut.

The van went dark. The chilled air was thick with the pungent smell of tomatoes.

When Molly woke up to find her mother lying in bed with her she squealed so loudly that it woke not just Maisie, but Tyler too.

'Mummy! Look Tyler, Mummy's here!' The little girl jumped up and down in the bed.

'Give us a kiss, my lovely girl.'

'Mum?' Tyler's voice sounded from the top bunk.

'Hello, love. I missed you so much I just came home.'

Maisie watched his feet appearing on the top rung of the step-ladder and then his legs, his pyjamas and then his face. Her own little boy, her beloved child. She hugged them both as tight as she could without hurting them.

'I just wanted to see you, is all.'

The door opened and Maisie's mum came in.

'You all right, love?'

She came over and stared down at her, Maisie met her gaze. Her mother could see what she could not say.

After breakfast Maisie emptied the bags of money she had sorted for Darcy onto the table.

'What's this?' Tyler said.

'Old money and London money.' She pushed it across the table. 'Help me sort it and then we'll go to the bank.'

Maisie drank her tea while Tyler sorted the coins. He was methodical, he sorted them by size and then arranged them all into piles. Maisie showed him what was Old money and what came from London. When he was done she totted it up. There was just the £23 of London money and, surprisingly, nearly £25 of Old money. It might be enough: prices for entertainment like cinema and ice skating had come down in the last years, otherwise people just could not afford to go.

'If we get enough let's go to Dreamland for the day.'

'Dreamland? Mummy, Dreamland. Can we go on the rides?'

'Yes, all of them. At least the ones you're big enough for.'

'What's Dreamland?' Molly said.

'It's like a big fairground', Maisie's mother said. 'It'll be lovely, a family day out. I'll make some sandwiches then.'

She got up and walked to the fridge.

'Thanks, Mum.' Maisie pursed her lip. She could feel the tears welling up all the time. She was lucky.

Steve was not sure if he was awake or asleep. If it was a nightmare it felt real, but how could he really be lying on a hard bunk in a cell. It had to be a dream. He closed his eyes. He had fallen asleep holding Tess, he could remember that. He could remember the feel of her skin, her smell, but that was before Norman had burst in. If Norman had barged in, that could be part of the nightmare. How could Norman have walked into his flat? and what kind of man offers you a whisky when your girlfriend is lying naked on the bed, unable to move, gagged and bound? That had to be a dream. He opened his eyes. Everything felt wrong.

The wall in front of him was shiny, it was a kind of gloss paint. Like bathroom paint, easy to clean. This was not his room, the poster of Dany was not on the wall, he was in something like a prison cell.

He sat up. His head hurt. He was wearing yesterday's clothes, except his trainers had no laces. There was nothing else in the room. It was bare. Just the thin plastic mattress on top of the built-in concrete bunk, the walls and ceiling a deathly pale grey, the floors green. He knew where he was, he was in a holding cell in Home Security.

This had to be a game. Not virtual reality, but role play. Why else would he be here? He tried to remember. Tess had arrived. They had eaten. They had made love. That was all clear. And then it got hazy. She wanted to be tied up, she wanted to be strangled. Then there was Norman. And drinking whisky. It was implausible. Then the nightmare of agents swarming into his room. Agents pulling him into a car. Tess's body not moving. She was cold and grey like the wall in here. It all seemed unreal, like VR, but the wall was cold; it was real.

He had no sense of time. He had slept again. They took him to an interview room. He had been in them before, taking notes. Now he was on the wrong side of the table. Gary Pierce walked in carrying a clutch of files. Steve said good morning to him every day when he passed his office, it was three doors before his. Gary did not look him in the eye.

'Hi, Gary.'

Gary stared at him.

'What's this all about? Is it some game?'

The guards who had walked him over had not spoken to him either. It was if they did not even want to touch him. Maybe they were keeping him in isolation because he was contaminated by something? Then he would be in a hospital.

'Stephen Foster?'

'Yes, Gary, you know it's me? What is this all about?'

'Do you really have no idea?'

'None.'

Gary rifled through the paperwork in one of the manila files.

'No one has deemed it necessary for you to see a psychiatrist, so I guess you're not mad. The question is whether you will confess and admit guilt.'

'To what?'

'Are you really going to play it like this?'

'I can't play a game if I don't know what it is, or what the rules are. Could you please tell me what is going on?'

'You have been arrested and taken into custody for two crimes.'

'Two crimes?' Steve racked his brain. It was so long since he had done any illegal hacking, and most of the websites he visited were legal. Or at least he went into illegal sites by way of TOR and the dark web. In theory, he left no trace.

'Yes, and we're not sure whether or how they are related.'

'This is mad? I'm a Home Security agent, not a criminal.'

'Which is why the first crime amounts to treason. We have evidence that you have been working as a mole in the Home Security with access to BiG computer networks and have been warning VNBs about impending Re-Migration.'

Gary pulled an A4 sheet of paper from the file and slid it over the desk. It was a photo of a man and a woman walking. The image looked familiar but different.

'Do you agree that is you?' Gary pointed his pen at the face of the man. Steve's face.

The head, the face, were his but the body was not, the clothes were not. Steve recognised the photo; it was the one he had shown Norman yesterday, but someone had transposed his face onto Mark Cooper's body.

'That's not me, it's Mark Cooper.'

'You deny it is you?'

'Yes, categorically.'

'And the woman?'

The woman had a different face as well. He had no idea who she was.

'I don't know who that is, but I know who it was?'

'Are you Yoda now?'

'It's Jenny Marshall, Norman's wife.'

He never knew that Gary was a boxer. The speed at which he sprung up and swung his fist into his face, before he could move, showed him that he was. Gary came around the desk and glowered down at him.

'You're scum. Norman Marshall has spent the morning ringing everyone asking for clemency for you. He has been on the phone ever since you were brought in, he has nothing but praise for you. He says you must have been set-up or blackmailed. And the first thing you do is attack him.' Gary sat down again.

'Yes, but...' There had never been any reason to think that Norman was smart, not in a treacherous, weasily way, but his bastard boss had stitched him up.

'Maybe people would have listened if it was not for the second charge.' Gary opened a second file.

'What's that?'

'The murder by strangulation of Tessa Jayne Webb.'

Steve closed his eyes, the dim memory of his arm over her cold body came to him.

'I wouldn't kill her. I love her.'

'Do you admit she was in your home last night?'

'Yes.'

'Do you admit you tied her to your bed, taped her mouth and strangled her with a black silk cord.'

'Yes, but she likes it like that. It was just for fun. She's into S&M.'

'And you're not?'

Steve did not answer. They could retrieve his search history on his PC.

'Do you admit you tied a black silk cord around her neck and tightened it with your own hands.'

'Yes, I did, but I didn't kill her.'

'We don't know yet if you fucked her before or after you killed her, but we know that you fucked her, that you strangled her and that she is dead. They're calling you the new Christie.'

'I didn't kill her.'

'We have video evidence of you strangling her for over a minute. We also have her corpse.'

'Video evidence?'

'Yes, you sick fuck, you shot your own snuff movie with your own webcam. You of all people should know, we can find what people hide on computers.'

Steve closed his mouth. There was nothing to say. Norman had warned him about the real world being dirty. Norman had chosen his wife over him, his wife over the country. He had been outplayed. Game over.

Alfie had been too frightened at first to go up the climbing frame. In the end, Tom had taken him by the hand and led him up there himself. Darcy watched her son exploring a playground for the first time. For the first twenty minutes he had not let go of her hand, she had had to climb the slide with him and he would only go down after Tom had slid down first. But the excitement of the other children seemed to infect him; she could almost see his fear slip away and soon he was chasing over the rope bridge and jumping down the slide like any other of the children spending Sunday morning in the park with their parents. She was sure that Alfie was the only one of them who had never seen any other children before.

The van driver had dropped them at a house in South London. A woman took them into her kitchen and asked if they knew anyone they could stay with while they got their paperwork in order. Tom had lost almost everything except the bank, credit and gym cards in his wallet. He needed new papers, a new passport, and then they could decide what to do. The woman drove them to his cousin's house. His cousin lived off Queensway and had suggested that they take Alfie down to Hyde Park. Now they were in the Princess Diana playground. Surreal. That was the word. The fear, the hiding, the gnawing anxiety just gone. Tomasz's cousin said they could stay while they worked out what to do; stay in London or go to Poland or even Brazil. Anywhere but back in the new Britain.

Alfie and Tom were running around a wooden sailing ship. Darcy stood and watched. Trailing after them on the ground as they sped over the wooden walkway. A week ago Tom had never met Alfie; a week ago she was picking strawberries; a week ago life was normal.

She sat down on a bench. Alfie ran up.

'Mummy, can we come back here every day?'

'Yes.'

'We're going to the swings.'

He charged off into Tomasz's hands, who picked him up and swung him high.

'This free?' A woman pointed at the other side of the bench.

'Yes, sure.'

The woman had three children. They kept running off and coming back again. The kids all had chestnut dark skin, their hair in tidy twisted rows. Children who would not pass as VB out there, who would live in fear, and here they were running free. They were in London. It was real. They were safe.

She wiped her eyes. It was just a tear, then a sob erupted from her mouth. She clamped her hand over it.

'Are you all right?' the woman reached over and patted her arm.

'I'm fine,' another sob came out, 'sorry, I'm just glad to be here. We've come from New Britain.'

'Oh,' the woman studied her, 'that little boy, is he yours?'

'Yes.'

'He'll be safe here.'

'I know, that's why I'm crying.'

She found Tom and Alfie at the swings. Tomasz wrapped her in his arms. She pressed her face against his chest and looked up.

'We'll be okay,' he whispered into her ear.

High above them a white vapour trail chased a tiny glint of silver through the blue sky. They could fly away.

The kids talked Maisie into getting off the bus at Westgate Bay and buying fish and chips for dinner. They had had, officially, the best day ever according to Tyler. Nobody wanted to go home. She could not remember a better day. The sun kissed their shoulders all afternoon, the breeze kept them cool. The queues were not too bad, they had gone on lots of rides and they even got a bus back without much of a wait. To cap it all a bench came free on the promenade over-looking the bay just as they walked past. A perfect end to a perfect day.

Molly and Tyler huddled down together and opened the cardboard box they were sharing. Tyler divided the food fairly.

Maisie sunk against the bench; the sea stretched out ahead, it just kept on coming in and going out. Nothing changed its tides. She pulled a bottle out of the paper bag.

'That's my chip. It was on my side,' Molly snatched one back from Tyler. He smiled.

Maisie took a swig of the beer. The cool, yeasty liquid slid down her throat. She took another swig.

'You want some?'

'Nah,' her mum said, 'you need to wind down.'

The sun was still higher than on a winter's day at noon. The air was balmy. She closed her eyes. It was like the last week had never happened. She had never got ants in her pants about Darcy, never gone snooping after her, her mum had never taken the kids down the beach, they had just had a normal week and a great day out. She opened her eyes. The sea was still frothing up onto the mudflats; it was beginning to go out.

'Mum?' Tyler's voice carried his hope on the wind.

'Yeah.'

'Can we go down onto the beach?'

'Ask Nan. She might be tired.'

'That'll be nice,' her mum said.

Maisie loved the way the sea rolled out quickly, unfurling almost as they walked up to it. The water left a fine sheen of silver over the wet sand. Sometimes, when the sun was low enough, the whole bay became a huge mirror; you could see clouds scudding over the flats. Not today, the sun was too high. The sky was still clear blue. The kids ran backwards and forwards like they always did, splashing in the tiny little streams that appeared in the sand. Picking up the odd stone and throwing it into the retreating waves. There were lots of people out with their dogs. This was just what she needed to get a perspective. She would go back to the farm tomorrow, act like nothing had ever happened. Just carry on like the sea, rolling in and out, on and on.

'Mum! Mum!' Tyler was running towards her. Holly fast behind.

Molly was crying.

'What's the matter,' Maisie tried to unpeel Tyler's arms from her legs, he was clinging tight.

'There are more of them.'

'More what?'

'More dead bodies,' her mother said as she looked to where Tyler and Molly had run from.

There were three bodies this time. Maisie started walking towards the nearest one, waves were tumbling over the other ones, they seemed smaller. As she walked towards them a fourth dark unmoving mass began to show through the retreating foam. Maisie stopped by the first body, it was a man's. He was lying face down. His hands were bound with a plastic tie behind him. She knew whose face she would see when she turned him over, she had seen Rohan Dhillon's picture often enough in the news. She stepped back.

The little girl's arms were stiff alongside her body. Maisie turned over the rigid corpse. Her face was bruised, any blood from the fall had been washed away. Maisie was used to picking her children up, they moulded into her arms, they were soft and compliant. Picking the girl up was like picking up a toddler in a tantrum. The little girl's body was inflexible and heavy. She left her mum standing over the other bodies. She had not put up much of an argument but had grasped Molly's hand in her own.

Tyler walked along in silence next to her. They reached the stairs leading up to the promenade and she put the dead girl down. Some people looking down over the railings.

'Should we call the police?' a woman shouted down.

'No, they did this.'

A dog started sniffing at the corpse lying on the sand. It was yanked back by a lead.

'What's going on?'

'Don't you recognise her?'

A crowd of people and their dogs was beginning to form around them.

'It's that girl they were looking for, isn't it?' a woman said.

'That's right. Her dad and her brothers are washed up on the beach down there.'

'I thought they were going to be reunited with their mum.' The woman got down and started to straighten out the dead girl's clothes.

'Yeah, right. Like the ones washed up on Birchington Beach last week; there was nothing about them in the news.'

'What do you mean?' the man with the dog said.

'What I mean is, this is Re-Migration.' Maisie was almost shouting, she swept her hand from the body to the beach in a wide arc. 'They chuck 'em out of an aeroplane and then they wash up on our sand. Where our kids are playing.'

Maisie looked at the faces of the people around her. They were all grim. Two teenagers were holding their phones up.

'Can you stream this live?'

She wiped a tear from her eye. 'Yeah.'

'Good. Everyone should know what's happening. There are three more bodies down there.' Her mother and Molly were still standing guard over the little heaps away down on the muddy flats. 'There's an empty grave where they dug up that painter Rossetti at the All Saints' graveyard in Birchington. Is anyone going to help me give them a decent burial? I'll need a car.'

Most of the people sloped off away down the beach, as if they had never seen or heard anything. The two girls stayed filming while Maisie walked back down the beach with two men and the woman. By the time they had the bodies up on the promenade there was a big crowd and many more people filming on their phones. Two men brought their cars round. The only way to get the children's stiff bodies in was to pile them on a back seat. It was a struggle to get the father into the reclined passenger seat of one of the cars.

'Get the kids home. I'll see these ones get a decent burial,' Maisie told her mum before she kissed Molly and Tyler and turned back to the waiting cars.

Jenny took the wine from the fridge. It was habit more than anything. She was sure she needed it. The lid unscrewed easily and she poured out a large glass of pale lemony liquid. She held the glass. She put it back down. She should turn the television on but some part of her resisted. She shut her eyes and groaned. She pulled her legs onto the sofa and extended herself the length of it.

'Oh my God!' she said aloud. 'Oh my God,' she said even louder. 'Mum!'

No one answered, there was no sound. The tears came then. She had barely thought about her mother since yesterday morning. She was gone. Debs and the children were gone. All she had now was Norman. The cat jumped onto her belly, it pivoted on the spot until it found the right way to sit down. It purred. She stroked the cat and let the tears flow down her cheeks onto the sofa.

When she woke up the cat was still there. She tried to sit up, the cat rolled off and jumped down. She picked up the remote control and turned the TV on. Last night they had watched Steve and Tess eating, drinking and making love. Then she had watched Steve pulling the cord round that poor woman's neck. What Norman did not know is that after he had turned the webcam off, she had turned it back on. He had told her to turn the camera off so there would be no trace of their meddling. She had ignored him, she had stopped only recording; she had wanted to know what he was prepared to do. She had watched him turn his head away as he had tightened the cord. He had counted aloud to 120. Then he had taken the pillow from under Tess's head and smothered her. Just one hand pressing the pillow down over her face, while he timed himself on his watch on the other wrist. Another two minutes of standing in silence. He was completely functional and proper, he put the pillow back under her head. Smoothed her hair. And then turned his back on her. Jenny had to force herself to shut the webcam down and then cover her tracks. She had typed in instructions, her fingers seemed to work on their own as her mind reeled in shock. She knew Norman was a killer, he was a soldier. But she had had no idea that man was a machine – he'd even apologised to Tessa before he strangled her – polite but with not a shred of emotion.

The TV screen woke up. She turned to the news channel. It was the sport news. Pictures of men in whites playing cricket on grass. The end of June and beginning of July was tricky for sports journalists. The NBBC could not pretend that Wimbledon was not happening, no more than they could give it any attention. Instead they showed wall to wall cricket and kept Wimbledon to bulletins. Neither BiG nor the NBBC could allow anything positive to come out of London.

She picked up her glass. The wine had lost its chill. She took a glug anyway. The headlines would be next.

There was a picture of a beach now and a crowd of people. The police were manhandling an angry woman into a car, she was shouting something again and again. Jenny wished she could lip read.

'Crowds gathered to cheer the police as they arrested a known terrorist, Maisie Wilson, in West Bay, Kent. Wilson was taken into custody for questioning about the abduction earlier this week of Rohan Dhillon and his three children.'

That was a lie. The people were jeering and holding up their phones. She froze the TV and typed in 'Maisie Wilson' in the search bar on her phone. She was the centre of a Twitter frenzy. She watched videos of Maisie Wilson carrying the corpses of two children up the beach, two men brought Rohan Dhillon and a woman brought his little boy. If they washed up on the shore they had either fallen from a boat or a plane. She wiped the tears from her face, they might still be alive if she had not intervened.

She pressed play again.

There it was. Steve was being taken out of his house in handcuffs, Steve being led into a court especially convened this afternoon. Norman had been called in as a witness. Then Rick McPherson standing on the court steps making an announcement.

'*It grieves me that it is one of my own trusted members of staff that will be taken to the gallows tomorrow. Yet it is fitting, as the nation returns to the time-honoured, punishment of a life for a life, that it should not be just a murderer but a traitor to the nation who should pay the ultimate price. It serves us all to remember that murder and treason are crimes against all of us. Steve Foster will pay the ultimate price for his crimes, let that be a lesson to us all. No one, whoever they work for, is above the law.*'

McPherson stepped away from the microphone and the newscaster carried on talking. All the while Norman had stood there his hands clasped in front of him, his face blank. As blank as when he had strangled Tess. Jenny felt sick. She was letting an innocent man die for her.

The screen filled with a wide shot of the gallows.

'*...first man or woman to be hanged since 1964.*'

She turned the TV off. Norman had made a few phone calls before he had gone to Steve's flat. He had never said what about. Someone had told someone to throw the Dhillons overboard. No one who knew about her treason would be alive after Steve was executed tomorrow. Norman was ruthless and thorough.

She drank the rest of the wine in a few gulps and reached for the bottle.

'To saving lives,' she raised the refilled glass.

There was little certain in this world. That Norman loved her she was sure, that certainty terrified her.

She needed her mother. Too late, her mother was dead. She picked up the glossy brochure for coffins the undertaker had given her as he had taken her mother away the day before. She flicked through the pages. Mahogany, wicker or cardboard; there were always choices to make.

Zero: Justice Day

At 6 a.m. this morning Steven Foster was executed at Gallows Park in central Birmingham. Convicted of treason against the state and murder of Re-Migration Camp Commander Tessa Webb, Foster was the first man to be hung in Britain since 1964. The Birmingham Metropolitan Police estimated that a crowd of six thousand gathered in the park to watch the hanging, while millions woke early to watch live from their televisions and phones.

Who's Who

In Birmingham, capital city of New Britain

Jenny Marshall née Chartridge, Britishness Verification Official/Resistance

Norman Marshall, BiG Home Security agent

Rohan Dylan né Dhillon, VNB (Verified Not British), sent for transit

Kirsty Dylan, Wife of Rohan, VB (Verified British)

Kiran Dylan né Dhillon, aged eight, son of Rohan & Kirsty, VNB

Maya Dylan née Dhillon, aged five, daughter of Rohan & Kirsty, VNB

Neel Dylan né Dhillon, aged two, son of Rohan & Kirsty, VNB

Mark Cooper, Britishness Verification Official/Resistance

Steve Foster, BiG Home Security IT forensics agent

Rick McPherson, BiG Home Security Commander

Meg Hunt, Britishness Verification Official

Simon Iverson, Driver, Re-Migration Services

In Kent

Cordelia Hughes, owner of C H Fruit Farms/Resistance

Tomasz Lisek, Foreman at C H Fruit Farms/Resistance

Maisie Wilson, Strawberry Picker at C H Fruit Farms

Liz Wilson, Maisie's mum, Birchington-on-Sea

Tyler Wilson, Maisie's son, aged five, Birchington-on-Sea

Molly Wilson, aged three, Maisie's daughter,
    Birchington-on-Sea
Darcy Knight, Strawberry Picker, Team Leader at C H Fruit
    Farms / Resistance
Alfie Knight, aged four, Darcy's son
Gill Knight, Darcy's mother
Sandy Melsom, Kent Socialite / Resistance
Lord Lopcombe, Chair of Kent Weald NFU
Keith Vicars, formerly Lieutenant Colonel in the Light
    Dragoons / Resistance
Tess Webb, Director, Ashford Re-Migration Transit Camp
Mick White, Tattooed Guard, Ashford Re-Migration Transit
    Camp / Resistance
Neil Seddon, Guard, Ashford Re-Migration Transit Camp
WPC Cotton, Margate Police Station

In Absentia
Dante Gabriel Rossetti, Pre-Raphaelite Painter, Poet, 1828–82,
    buried at Birchington-on-Sea
Jay, Maisie's former partner, fled to St Lucia
Jayde, Maisie and Jay's daughter, in St Lucia
Ray Hughes, Cordelia's brother, in Brazil
Luis, Ray's stepson, in Brazil

Acknowledgements

This book could not have been written without the failure of the British political establishment. I cannot thank them here as tradition would require but I can acknowledge their contribution to the creative process. There should never have been a referendum. The UK should not be in the situation it finds itself in as I write this. The complete lack of trust, sense of hopelessness, disbelief in experts, rejection of facts, figures and hard news has shaped both the outcome of the vote and the response to it.

When argument and logic, facts and figures fail to change people's minds, fail to persuade us from entrenched positions there is another way: stories. Stories can captivate, convince, and coax in a way that political rhetoric and expert discourse cannot. I have written a story, that I hope is plausible, of how things could go if we suffer the hardest of Brexits and it brings out the worst in us. It is not far-fetched. It is not hard to imagine. I hope I am wrong.

There are many people to thank. I could not have written this without the support and help of Farah Ahmed, Don Clark, Christina Dunhill and Howard Lester – my writing group; Marion Regan spent a day showing me everything I needed to know about strawberry production, giving this book its heart; Mark Bowers helped me in the gallows design – it's so handy when the cake-making, rowing teenager grows up to be a Senior Engineer in Materials, Advanced Technology and Research at a leading international firm; Joshua Harry Brown took on the photographic commission for the website with such insight, I wish I could have used all his images; Kira Gurmail Kaufman designed the perfect noose. Paul Brooks, Carolyn Fairbairn, India Gurmail Kaufmann, Raffael Jovine, Nick Kaufmann, Tracey Matthias, Anna Robinson Pant, Leigh Turner and Richard Wolfe read various drafts, their comments and thoughts reshaped the final version; Keir Starmer and Anand Menon for trying; Howard Lester created the website and made that terrifying prospect fun; Mark Ecob designed the book cover that brilliantly captured my ideas, while fielding my over-excitement with grace; Elspeth Sinclair endured my inability to punctuate and tidied the text; and last but not least Richard, Ruth and Hannah who tolerated my neglect and obsessiveness.

G. L. Kaufmann lives in London. She left a career as an anthropologist to pursue her childhood dream of writing. *A Hard Fall* is the novel she wished she did not have to write.

If you want to get a further taste of
the New Britain, 2025 take a look at:
https://www.ahardfall.uk/

MULBERRY PUBLISHING

www.mulberrypublishing.co.uk

If there is time and opportunity
https://www.peoples-vote.uk/